T0161346

THE TRIAL OF
FATHER DILLINGHAM

THE TRIAL OF
FATHER DILLINGHAM

a novel by
JOHN BRODERICK

Marion Boyars
London · Boston

*Published simultaneously in Great Britain and the United States
in 1982 by
Marion Boyars Ltd.
18 Brewer Street, London W1R 4AS*

*and by
Marion Boyars Inc.
99 Main Street, Salem, New Hampshire 03079*

*Australian and New Zealand distribution by
Thomas C. Lothian
4-12 Tattersalls Lane, Melbourne, Victoria 3000*

© John Broderick 1982

British Library Cataloging in Publication Data
Broderick, John
   The trial of Father Dillingham.
   I. Title
   823'.914[F]   PR6052.R/
ISBN 0-7145-2747-5

Library of Congress Catalog Card Number 81-52333

Photoset by E.B. Photosetting Ltd, Woodend Avenue, Speke, Liverpool
and printed in Great Britain by
Redwood Burn, Trowbridge, Wilts.

to
Julian Green

Everyone was a little someone else.

(From *The Great Good Place* by Henry James)

Prologue:
Yesterday's Newspaper

Excerpt from a review by Rose Mann in the book page of the *Irish Times*, Saturday, 17th November 1966

Mr Denison's thought-provoking argument is briefly thus: the claims of the classical doctrine of original sin are too arbitrary, too neatly packaged to tie up with an enormous edifice of largely ambiguous theological concepts. Modern man could not accept the proposition that all the pain and suffering in the world came about through the disobedience of first parents. The story of Genesis is meaningful and profound; but as an explanation of the beginning of things it is so patently absurd that modern exegetists have been forced to put it forward as a symbolic story of the end of things; a Garden of Eden which corresponded to the longings of man in some future state, rather than a paradise from which they had been expelled for some trifling disobedience, the exact nature of which nobody knows. Newman's 'terrible aboriginal calamity' was a very vague premise: poetic, but not very informative.

It would appear that the authors of Genesis, filled with primitive religious fervour and fully aware of the disorder of the human condition, had developed their concept of sin to fit in with their limited knowledge of the race. They could have had no inkling of the process of evolution, and, accustomed to think in strictly moral and legalistic terms, explained man's animal nature in the context of disobedience. This early discovery of original sin gave much scope to the legal mind, which interpreted everything in black and white, and encouraged a sense of guilt in all believers. The dogma of some vague, unspecified fall became the cornerstone of a vast theology of sin and redemption. The Catholic Church developed the idea, played down the humanity of Christ for many centuries, and laid an undue emphasis on fear and guilt. The ferocious doctrine of St Augustine was a logical extension of this; but was discovered to be so pitiless that it has now withered away. Yet the concept of original sin, which few understand, has remained because so many elaborately constructed theological theories rest upon it. It gives an entirely false slant to the real mission of the Church, which is the doctrine of love, not fear.

Evolution has made things a little clearer for us. No infallible claims are now made for special creation, although it is horrifying to contemplate that for many centuries men could be put to death for daring to question it.

What does not seem to have occurred to any theologian, obsessed as they are by the need to prove the necessity of atonement, is that all the pain, confusion and injustice in the world are not the result of some fall, before which all was delightful, but the natural consequence of our animal nature, which did not need any sin of disobedience to make it brutal. We are all animals with souls; hence our longing for some future state of perfection, and our instinctive recognition of good. We have evolved out of the slime and primeval forest, and our lowest impulses are still those of beasts. What we carry within us is not the guilt of some misguided first parent, but the mark of the beast.

12

Christ came certainly to redeem us, to point out that we are capable of surmounting the savage within us and purifying our basest instincts by love. He raised us up, not from guilt and fear, but from ignorance. He preached the doctrine of tolerance, self-denial and restraint, the very opposite of the law of the jungle to which we are all heirs by reason of our long ferocious struggle for survival. This natural law selects only the cunning, the ruthless and the strong as leaders. Christianity, with its insistence on love for the weak, the sick and the oppressed, is the opposite of all this. Original sin is a state of ignorance for which we cannot be held responsible. Christianity is the rule of love and order, to ignore which is to turn away from our supernatural destiny.

There is much food for thought here; and at least one reviewer burned the midnight oil ...

Faith Without Guilt by Mark Denison. Cantor and Cooper, 30/-

Part One

I

They were all late.

Jim Dillingham stood at the window of his flat and looked down on the square. He had written to Eddie and Maurice from Rome a week before telling them of the day of his arrival. His plane for once made it on time, and he had been expecting Maurice since shortly after five. Eddie was sometimes delayed at the office, and was moreover a notorious dawdler; but in the ten years that he had lived in the same house with him, Jim never knew Maurice O'Connell to be late for anything. It was now half-past six. Either his letter had gone astray, or something was wrong.

The La he kept posted with colourful cards, especially from Milan and Vienna, the scenes of her former triumphs; but he had not told her the day of his arrival, as he wanted to slip in quietly, unpack and rest a little before facing the drama of her welcome home scene.

Besides he knew from the little notes which she sent him posts restante in the various cities he visited that the La was her usual blooming self, whereas Eddie's last two letters were curiously stilted and evasive: he was obviously worried about something. Maurice had not written at all, but then Maurice never wrote to anyone. As the hours slipped by in the empty house he became filled with a vague disquiet.

Below him the street lights waxed the trees in the small railed-in park in the centre of the square. It had been a long mild autumn; and when he arrived shortly after lunchtime, the yellowing beeches and chestnuts had as yet dropped few leaves on to the sunken pavement outside the railings, while dull patches of green still survived among the foliage.

There was a momentary lull in the purring traffic below: one of those sudden silences which even now gives the illusion of time regained in the few Dublin squares that retain most of their facades intact. Jim was aware of a feeling of abeyance, such as he sometimes experienced after awakening from a heavy sleep. He leaned forward and narrowed his eyes, his shoulder brushing against the velvet curtain. Over the shimmering trees lights were glowing behind blinds in the upper stories of the tall Georgian houses; isolated irregular patches scattered here and there above the darkened windows of the ground floors, now occupied mostly by doctors and insurance companies. Each year the number of lights in the upper windows dwindled at night as the companies spread their tentacles aloft, and a new section of one of the government departments, already scattered all over the city, moved in. Last winter, before he went abroad, he noticed one evening that the house he lived in on the east side of Fitzwilliam Square, was the only one left entirely occupied by private persons.

An ambulance shrieked by; and the fading illusion was shattered. He turned away from the window and thrust his hands into his pockets. For want of something better to do he pulled out their contents, and saw the envelope of the message that Desmond and Grace had phoned through and left for him at the airport. He opened it and peered into the dark corners of the big room, lit now only by the street lamps. His eye caught the drab blob of white like a dirty shirt thrown over the arm of the sofa in front of the fireplace. It was the newspaper he had bought at Collinstown. There was no need to reconstruct the small headline or the blurred photograph which was reproduced underneath it. 'Retirement of Bishop'. It was not a recent likeness, and must have been taken about ten years before: when they had last met, 1966.

He had been surprised by the emotions which succeeded one another as he read the piece in the bus coming into the terminal. Disbelief. Ten years could not have passed so quickly. The old man was seventy-five; but then in Jim's eyes he had always been old. No mention was made of ill-health; and it was difficult to believe that the Bishop welcomed the new regulations with enthusiasm, least of all the idea of handing over the reins to anybody. Regret. For the passing of the years? For what had happened? A

18

mixture of both, perhaps. He did not allow himself to think about it too much. What was over was done with.

Carefully he crossed the shadowy room to the switch. Galvanized by light he strode back and drew the curtains on the two windows. Then he went over to the mantelpiece and examined the ornaments: the silver snuff-boxes, the candle-sticks, the pair of blackened Russian ikons, and the collection of coloured crystals which seemed frivolous until one noticed the two miniature ivory skulls set among them. They silenced more than one gushing admirer; and were equally effective with cynics.

But he was merely marking time. Maurice had a key of the flat; The La could not get in: everything was in its place, and nothing was missing. What the hell was the matter with him? He walked restlessly over to the telephone which stood on a half-table under the light-switch, and shook out the message while he was dialing Grace's number. 'Welcome home. Give us a ring when you have time. Love. Desmond and Grace'.

The telephone buzzed for quite a while before Grace answered it herself. She sounded breathless and recognized his voice at once.

'I got your message,' he began rather lamely, 'so I thought I'd ring and thank you. I hope I haven't disturbed you.'

'I was just getting out of the bath. Desmond is still soaking. I thought I wouldn't get to the telephone in time. We're going out to dinner.' Having recovered her breath Grace was her old self again, calm, soft-voiced, imperturbable. Jim felt faintly irritated.

'How is everybody?' Grace sounded faintly preoccupied. He could imagine her clutching a bath-towel over her breast as she talked.

'I don't know. There's nobody here. They're all out.'

There was a slight pause.

'What a pity we're going out,' she went on smoothly. 'We'd have dropped in to hear all the news.'

He said nothing, waiting.

'How was Europe?' she went on. 'Very small?'

19

'Very, now.'

'And the notes? Very large?'

He glanced over his shoulder at the bulging brief-case lying like a bloated bull-dog on one of the chairs.

'Yes.'

'And the flat? Nothing missing, I hope.'

'No. I left the key with Maurice. The La couldn't get in.'

'I expect she's being escorted home by some blushing young Guard.' Grace laughed. 'What a clever technique. I often wondered how much of it was calculated.'

There was clearly no future in this conversation. Grace was not going to talk about Eddie or Maurice. After a few banalities, during which Grace promised to ring him in a day or two, he put down the receiver and gazed slowly about the room, his large dark eyes, usually so disconcerting with their piercing expression, heavy with fatigue. There was nothing to do but check up on his unpacking. He opened drawers, desks and the wardrobe, finding everything in its place, except the briefcase, which he unlocked and emptied, putting the thick block of type-written notes in the top left-hand drawer of his desk between the windows. The packet of octavo on which he would collate the notes and sketch out the first draft of his book was lying unopened in the right-hand drawer.

He occupied the first floor of the house. It consisted of the great L-shaped drawing room, divided in two by folding doors. These were usually kept closed, since he used the back portion as a bedroom; but tonight they were drawn back as he moved to and fro, unpacking. The front was quietly but comfortably furnished: an old, subtly coloured Persian carpet, the fine Regency desk, and an enormous book-case reaching almost to the ceiling at the end of the room facing the marble fireplace. Books were everywhere, on tables, chairs and cabinets.

In contrast the bedroom was stark. A single iron bed covered with a white quilt; a dressing table and wardrobe, two bentwood chairs, and an ebony crucifix with a silver figure of Christ on the wall over the night table. The fireplace, of equal magnificence to the one in the front, was

20

completely bare of ornaments. The floor was waxed and polished, covered with two rugs; one against the brass fender, the other beside the bed. Beyond this bare apartment were a bathroom and kitchenette.

Jim sat down on the arm of the sofa and rubbed his chin. He had shaved at six that morning in Amsterdam, and his lean cheeks bristled under his fingertips. The silence in the curtained room was oppressive. It seemed to him that all his life was contained and concentrated here. Everything that had happened in the last ten years he was seeing and feeling here and now. The four books in their various translations in the corner of the shelves. The anxiety over the three people who were late, bringing home to him how few friends he had, and what reliance he placed upon them. The note from Grace and Desmond, his only link with that submerged part of his life that changed so completely on his arrival in Dublin. They were an easy undemanding link, that pair; but the stern old face that looked up at him from the newspaper was another matter. That brought those other ten years of his adult life flooding back with almost unbearable force: a mountain pool from the front of which a rock had been dislodged.

He stood up abruptly, folded the paper and thrust it into a drawer. Then he went into the bedroom, opened the locked wardrobe where only a few hours previously he had deposited the little silver phial, which he replenished from time to time, always on the continent or in London. He weighed it in his hand, closed his eyes for a moment in utter weariness, then put it back and locked it again.

Picking a detective story at random from the book shelves, he settled down on the sofa to read and wait. The clock on the mantelpiece ticked gently on – the heating was turned up; Maurice had forgotten nothing. But where was he? And why should it be that he, Jim Dillingham, who always prided himself on his inflexible self-control, now felt such an overwhelming desire to take the phial out again and pour its contents down the sink?

21

II

The piped music was playing a selection of Cole Porter. At the moment the muted strings were crooning out 'Everytime we say Good-bye'. Friday was Cole Porter night at the Rainbow Inn. Saturday evening was given over to the tunes associated with Judy Garland and Marlene Dietrich. But Eddie Doyle did not know this. He had never been in the place before – although he was well aware of the special reputation it enjoyed in the half-world of Dublin – and he passed it every afternoon on his way home from work. It was near the corner of Baggot Street Bridge, not far from the bookshop and newsagent at the corner of Mespil Road where he bought his papers, books and stationery.

He worked in Ballsbridge as press-agent and part-time secretary to the director of Irish Grain Importers. He always walked home from the office, down Pembroke Road to the canal.

'Does that tune get you below the belt?' inquired the man whose name was Abraham Gillespie.

'What?' said Eddie vaguely, lifting his glass and looking round the bar.

The other was puzzled and in his dull, slow way even a little hurt. There were only two others in the place when the small, fair-haired man came in a little after five. Not that Eddie was all that small – he was of medium height and had unusually broad shoulders – but Abraham, who was six feet three and built like a Cretan bull, thought of most of the rest of the world as physically inferior to himself. The stranger's neat blue business suit did not altogether conceal his plumpness; but his face with its slightly undershot mouth was clear skinned and still untouched by muzziness.

'Mild weather for this time of year,' Abraham had remarked as insinuatingly as his sandpaper Dublin voice would allow. In the background the far-off strings were playing 'Always True to you in my Fashion'. The newcomer's response was immediate. He gave a shy but friendly smile, a small white hand was raised, and a clear precise voice caused the first of a long row of pints to be set in front of the delighted connoisseur of the national beverage.

After another drink they moved to a table in the corner to the strains of 'Get out of Town'. Eddie talked, quietly at first, and then with growing animation, while Abraham listened with deep attention only half feigned. This was not the usual bird-like chatter to which he had become accustomed on the part of gentlemen who bought him drinks in the Rainbow Inn.

As he listened and the glasses lined up in front of him Abraham watched the other's mobile face and nodded gravely from time to time, without attempting to understand much of what was being said. But he was aware of a dim feeling of admiration, and a baffled consciousness of his own inadequacy.

'What was that you were saying?' Eddie leaned forward with a smile and looked into the blank, wondering eyes.

'Nuttin. I was just saying deffly. You have the point there deffly.'

'That's a real Dublin one.' Eddie lifted his finger, and Abraham frowned at the barman's smirk. It was as fine a tribute as he could pay to his companion.

'Deffly. It definitely is.' Abraham pronounced the word slowly and exactly, just to show that he knew how the rest of the world dealt with it.

Eddie smiled and lifted his glass in response to Abraham's toast, then set it down again without drinking. The other watched him over the top of his foaming Guinness. Not once since he came into the bar had Eddie looked about him. He did not seem to possess that 'over-the-shoulder' eye so characteristic of the regular habitues of the place in big Abe's experience. The docker felt the beginning of a warm glow, and not just because of the Guinness.

Every Friday, after receiving his pay packet, he washed himself, got into his brown suit and suede shoes and made for the Rainbow. It was a complete philosophy of life, personified but never expressed. What good were labels? You could change them about and nobody could tell the difference. And here there was always someone to buy him drinks, and listen to him with a kind of respectful awe, in spite of the flickering eye and the shrill asides which accompanied such encounters. But this attentive stranger was different. Abraham would not have minded seeing a lot more of him. It was the first dim formulation of names; the beginning of confusion.

'Miss Otis Regrets' spilled softly from the loudspeaker and a few more regulars came into the place. But it was early yet. The Rainbow did not really come alive until about ten.

Eddie had not come here in search of pleasure or even of company, but as a kind of desperate remedy, as a man will revert to quackery after being given up by the doctors. Perhaps back here in this world where it had all begun, somehow miraculously all would be well. But the experiment had not killed the pain.

'Don't Fence Me In'. The Rainbow had been the 'in' bar for the past two or three years. But apart from its decor and its situation, it was exactly the same as all the others he had known in the years before he met Maurice. The same smell of soft masculinity; the same tense watchfulness; the undercurrent of slightly hysterical violence; the bright sadness. All this assailed him as he looked around. It was in just such a place that they first met twelve years before. In those days it had been 'The Bloomsday' off Grafton Street.

And then in the mirror behind the bar he saw the door open and a man come in. A tall, dark-faced man with greying hair, brown sunken eyes and a wide harsh mouth. Eddie started so violently that he upset his glass, and Abraham, anxious to please, clucked his tongue and leaned over to set it up. The stranger met Eddie's eye in the glass and turned away. The resemblance was not on second glance very close, but it was enough to finish that doomed pilgrimage. 'I Get a Kick out of You'.

24

'Antin up?' said Abraham with clumsy sympathy, as he mopped up the gin with his handkerchief. He would not do that for everybody. Deffly not.

Eddie stared back at him. Abraham, aware of something lost and inexplicable in that inspection, wiped the foam from his upper lip with his handkerchief and tasted spirits as surely as earlier he thought he had tasted blood. Where was the difference? But Eddie recovered himself.

A moment after he felt ashamed. Impulsively he leaned across the glasses and touched Abraham's sleeve, unaware that without gentleness cruelty would have little meaning.

'I'm sorry. I've got to go. Have a ball of malt.'

Before the other could reply he stood up, went to the counter, ordered the drink and paid for it. Then he hurried out to the strains of 'What is This Thing Called Love?'

III

He stopped at the bottom of Leeson Street, waiting for the traffic lights to change, then crossed with a couple of others to the island and reached the gates of the park, now closed for the night. Yes, Isaacson had been right about Dublin. St Stephen's Green with its mixture of Georgian mansions, gleaming new banks and office blocks, and blank gaping spaces where old buildings had been pulled down and new ones about to be erected, did look like a vacant film lot. In one corner they might have been making a glossy comedy-drama about the hucksters of big business, in another, an eighteenth-century epic, and in the boarded-up sites, a spy thriller set among the ruins of Berlin. Indeed a few years previously they had made just such a film in Dublin.

Maurice O'Connell had always been a great walker, especially as a young man. There were few corners of Dublin which he did not know, yet he remained a provincial. When he first came to the city at the age of eighteen in the war years, the traffic had been light, and the Georgian squares and streets still had an aura of another age. These had been the lonely years; the nights of the long walks, the time of the terrible breakthrough to the reality of his own nature, and the still more terrible consequence of its acceptance. Then indeed, Dublin, with its high, flat parapets concealing the roofs from the restless watcher in the streets, had seemed very blank indeed: an unreal, theatrical place in which everybody played a part, and most of all himself.

He realized, as he turned down into Grafton Street, that on this walk he was retracing the scenes of most of his life in the city. He had started as a shop boy in Clerys, and had digs in the North Circular Road. Three ten a week, and thirty-five bob for the shared room with two others. But after a few years he moved across the bridge to the south side, and had remained there ever since, first in Brown

Thomas in the shoe department, later in a wholesale warehouse in William Street, and finally in the shoe shop in Grafton Street where he was now manager. He passed it without a glance at the windows which he had supervised last Monday. A tall, ruddy-faced Guard was standing in the doorway, rubbing his gloved hands. For a moment Maurice thought it was Greg Hughes, and remembered Eddie. He would surely be home now in time to break the news to Jim, and welcome him back.

He looked across at Brown Thomas and Duke Street, and the past came flooding back again. A nice sight he must have looked in those days in that soft-toned shop. The big, awkward, red-handed young man, with the wild mop of curly black hair, the pock-marked gypsy skin, and the brown eyes that even then were losing their soft, lost expression.

Duke Street and The Bloomsday. Now cleaned up and impersonal, a mecca for tourists, and a few middle-aged men who dated themselves by their loyalty to their old haunt, it brought back memories of the bad days to Maurice. The eight lost hopeless years when he had taken to drink with a violence only found in men of an essentially puritan character. How he kept his job during that time he had never since been able to understand. But like all alcoholics he was as strong as a bull. No matter how bad the hangover, or the frantic encounters of the previous night, he rarely missed a day's work. And then suddenly he gave it up, completely and forever; the only way that men like him can do anything. He had relapsed into a kind of limbo, unfeeling, apathetic, going about his work with mechanical precision, resigned to a dull repetition of predictable days and nights. A lonely man in a lonely room, with a few books and records and a secret contempt for all mankind, especially himself.

And then one day, when his black hair was already turning grey, and the bitter lines settled about his mouth, he had gone into The Bloomsday on the prowl, half-crazed with loneliness, ordered a tonic water, and met Eddie Doyle. The miracle had happened. How rare it was

27

both of them knew. Twelve years ago; the slow thawing of his suspicions; the move to the flat in Fitzwilliam Square; the meeting with Desmond and Grace; the enlargement of his world, vicariously on his part, through an acquaintance with their set. The La, Jim Dillingham; the long quiet years that followed. Was he paying for all that now? For his whole life, or only one half of it? And which half?

These memories flitted but lightly through his mind as he turned into Nassau Street, for he was not given to nostalgia. All he knew at that moment was that he would get no further than the taxi rank in Molesworth Street and drive home, short as the distance was. All the walk had produced was a rapid skate over thin ice, under which dark waters lurked. It was in its way an exercise as futile and superficial as Eddie's visit to The Rainbow. Ahead lay the real trial, the final settling of accounts. Neither of them ever consciously asked themselves why they both associated this with Jim Dillingham.

IV

Nevertheless, it was The La who got there first. She swept
into Jim's flat and enfolded him in her arms, almost
smothering him with the scent of Roman Hyacinth, the
essence of which, by Floris, she bathed in, and the perfume
of which she liberally sprinkled all over her ample person.

'Caro mio!', she cried, standing back with her arms still
outstretched, and peering at him mistily with her great
gentian blue, short-sighted eyes. Not for her to feel remorse
for the two big blobs of scarlet lipstick which she had
smudged on both his cheeks, leaving him looking, as he
knew from past experience, like a sadly inefficient clown.
'You return. Io so che alfine reso me sei! I knew it, I knew
it. Last night I dreamed of the death of a horrible critic in
Milano who hated me because I would not sleep with him.
No, no, never. And to dream of a death is to hear of the
living, and I have heard of all of the living I know already,
so I knew you were returning.'

She threw off her old mink coat, and flung it in the
general direction of a chair, where it slipped and fell to the
ground, giving Jim the opportunity while lifting it to lick his
fingers and run them hastily over his cheeks. He did not
know whether this made him look better or worse; but after
all who was there to see except Maurice and Eddie, and
they would understand.

'You look wonderful, Maria,' he said as quietly as he
could, for he was always as happy as a little boy to see her
again. 'What have you been doing with yourself?'

She closed her eyes with their long thick lashes, and drew
in a long rapturous breath, as if she were smelling roses.

'Having tea in Jonathan's with the new attache at the
Italian Embassy, Jachimo mio. Divine, divine, like Tito
Pignatelli used to look like, oh a hundred years ago. Only
this one's father makes spokes for bicycles in Torino, or
something like that. But he has learned, that one. He kissed

29

my hand in the Roman fashion. But enough of him, the beautiful animal. Tell me everything. Is Leoni still in the Eden? No, no, but of course he isn't. I hear all that at the Embassy. He is dead, they are all dead. There is nothing that you can tell me. I don't want to hear. I had the best of it. And Wien too. I hear it is all Wagner and Strauss, Richard, at the Staatsoper now. Not a decent woman who can sing Italian. Even as well as Jeritza, which is not saying much. Gott im Himmel, how long ago it all was.'

The La smoothed her green velvet dress, the second best one, and held out her still beautiful hand, small, white and pointed, to admire her great emerald, sole genuine relic of her great days. The advent of costume jewellery had been a gift from heaven to her. She was hung about with a load of gold chains, medallions and bracelets which looked heavy enough for a circus pony, but which had not cost more than five pounds. She touched her bright yellow hair, pursed out her lips, narrowed her glistening eyes and took stock of herself in the mirror. There were times when her short-sightedness was a balm to the heart, and she could still imagine herself the raving beauty she had once been: the wild, blue-eyed, blonde Irish prima donna, who left a trail of broken hearts (easily mended) behind her in her triumphant progress through the Italian opera houses in the thirties. Even now, at seventy, she was still handsome with her peach-blossom skin, enchanting smile and irresistible gaiety.

She was born plain Mary Jane Kelly in Castlebar, and had not a single relative left in the world, in spite of the fact that she claimed with some justification that every Kelly in Mayo pretended to be a cousin of hers, after she made her name as the greatest Irish singer since McCormack. On the strength of a scholarship young Mary Jane had gone from the R.A.M. in London to the Boito Conservatorio in Parma, and afterwards as a private pupil to Carmen Melis. A short but brilliant career followed. Six seasons at the Scala, one under Toscanini, in Vienna and Berlin, a couple of appearances at Covent Garden and the Paris Opera, one at the Metropolitan, Vienna again before the Anschluss, and back to her beloved Italy. Then the war, and a sudden return to Ireland and complete retirement, for she would not sing in her own country. A host of myths had grown up about this early retirement, the most persistent being the one about the Roman prince who committed suicide because she would not marry him, after which she had a nervous breakdown. Only a few people, including Desmond and Grace, knew the real reason: the gleaming top notes grew unreliable and would not always come when they were called. She preferred to retire before the legend was exploded.

On her debut she changed the spelling of her name to Keeley, and dropped the Jane. It looked better that way; besides, that was how the Italians pronounced it. She was known to all Ireland as Madame Keeley, and to the cynical Dubliners as The La. No one knew better than she how to play the prima donna when the occasion arose, but the nick-name was affectionate. La Keeley was the real thing in spite of her short career, one of the greatest Mimis, Cio-cio-sans and Desdemonas of her day, and her records were there to prove it. Every year or two Radio Eireann had a programme – for the Irish never forget a celebrity who has made the grade abroad – and requests for the few records she had made of Moore's melodies were as numerous as those for McCormack.

Now she took a step nearer Jim, raised her head and inhaled deeply.

'You smell the same,' she said gravely, pressing her fore-finger against her cheek and cocking her head sideways. 'Nothing has changed with you, I know. Pine wood, fresh pine wood, and sometimes like when one opens a new book. I knew it at once when I came in. If I had not dreamed last night, I would still have known you were back.' The La was a great one for smells and held that they were a surer guide to character than faces, movements, or even the palm on which she was an authority. Eddie smelled of roses, and Maurice of leather, Grace of fresh linen, and Desmond of apples – slightly rotten at the core she would add when in a delphic mood.

31

'I stink,' said Jim, moving away from her. 'I haven't washed since last night. And I haven't had a bath since I got in.'

'You have unpacked.' She looked around quickly, screwing up her eyes.

'Yes, hours ago. I was ...,' he stopped short and bit his lip.

From the quick flicker of understanding that darted across her eyes he knew that she realized what he was about to say. But she was not an actress for nothing.

'But you haven't eaten,' she exclaimed, clapping her hands. 'You look famished. I have veal and paprika in the fridge, and I know Eddie has lemons. Mamma mia, does he not know that I can smell it through a locked door. I will make Wiener Schnitzel for you better than Otto at the Sacher.' She closed her eyes, threw out her hands and relapsed into the broadest Mayo. 'Jasus, Mary and Joseph, I suppose he's dead too. Did you get any kind of material for the auld book? God knows, you were long enough away, so you were. In that time if I had the power of the pen I'd have written "War and Peace" backwards in double Dutch.'

But Jim was not going to be put off. He chuckled and shook his head. She had given him an opportunity. Was it intentional? One never knew with The La.

'No lemon. Eddie isn't back yet. At least I don't think so.'

'Do you have to tell me that?' she demanded with mock indignation. She gazed down at her gleaming emerald and studied it for a moment. When she looked up her expression had changed. She allowed her face to sag, something she never did when she was acting. Under the mask of sophistication, the peasant features suddenly became apparent: the high cheek bones, the broad base of the nose, fatalistic sadness in the eyes. It was an expression which Jim had seen only two or three times before, for she rarely displayed it except in the privacy of her own flat, when she was alone with the all-too-certain future. She might have been an old woman, perhaps her own grand-mother, sitting in the corner, thinking of nothing and sure only of death in her bones.

'Neither of them are back,' she said quietly. 'I know that, just as I knew you'd be here. But you wrote to them, telling them when you were coming, and they aren't here. You men are such children, playing hide-and-seek with me, thinking you can fool me. I've fooled more men in my time than ...' she broke off and shrugged. Living together under the same roof, knowing one another as well and as little as a family, The La and her small brood had evolved their own code, light, discreet and quite complicated.

Jim felt guilty, and not for the first time. It was difficult to know exactly how to treat The La in the matter of social nicities. Understanding, on a deeper level, was different.

'Is anything wrong?' he asked bluntly.

She turned, reached out for a chair and sank heavily into it, clasping her knuckles and twiddling her thumbs on her lap. She had grasped the first chair, not the usual Louis XV armchair which she usually chose, contriving to turn it into a throne. Nor had her expression changed.

'Maurice is sick. And he isn't going to get better. They haven't told me that either, of course. Not even Grace. But I know.'

Jim sat down by the fireplace and felt his stomach turn and rumble from shock and lack of food. But he was too stunned to be embarrassed. In the hours that he had been waiting several possibilities for the delay had occurred to him. The usual hazards that accompany lives that are vulnerable: blackmail, money trouble, a sudden ending to a long and not altogether easy friendship. In face of it La Keeley reverted to type, and behaved with the courage and delicacy of the full-blooded old country woman she was. One does not want to be the first to break bad news to a home-coming traveller. An ancient code, which Maurice and Eddie were also obviously following. But The La had also the courage of her kind. When faced with the harsh truth she did not evade it.

But there was more to it than that. What was he supposed to revert to now? He looked at the old woman sharply, but she glanced away and twisted her ring slowly. He felt a sudden chill panic as the first segment of a pattern which he could dimly perceive fell into place.

'What is it?' he asked softly.

She did not answer, but rose from her chair and stood facing the door which she had left open in her excitement. With ears keener than his she heard a noise in the hall. Someone had returned.

V

It was Maurice. He would have to pass the door on his way to the top flat. They listened to his slow heavy steps, a series of mounting thuds on the thin old carpet. The La looked at Jim and shook her head. He was to give no sign of surprise when he saw Maurice. She lifted her own chin and smiled: the years, the hidden sadness and fatalism dropped away from her, and the chair became a throne once more.

Instinctively Jim jumped to his feet and hurried to the door, prepared to make a fuss. It was easier that way; and he had had enough time to steel himself for the encounter. He darted out into the landing and caught the shadowy figure by the arm.

'Well, you old bear, where have you been?' he demanded, drawing him into the room where The La was already playing her part; a benign queen presiding over the meeting of two of her warriors, both baritones.

Maurice grimaced, a sort of relaxed wince that was peculiar to him. That had not changed. He had never been the smiling sort. Even his rare laughter had a harsh note which The La often likened to the tuning up of an amateur orchestra.

'Welcome back, stranger,' he said in his slow, grudging drawl, looking into Jim's face with a defiant glance before peering round the room with his dark sunken eyes. 'That tan suits you. You don't look as if you spent all your time in the archives. How is the Pope? Still dithering like an old hen?'

'That's enough of that,' Maria tapped the arm of her throne sharply with her long crimson nails. She was inclined to exaggerate her piety, which was genuine, but intermittent. Besides, had she not sat at the same table as Monsignor Montini at the Palazzo Colonna in Rome? It was not every opera singer who could boast of that. She had been a good girl during her Italian years, although there were times when she told a very different story.

Maurice grunted, and began to take off his coat slowly, giving the others time to exchange a quick glance. Jim was shocked at the change in Maurice. The big, heavily boned man, who had always given the impression of enormous physical strength liable to turn to brute violence at any moment, was shrunken almost to emaciation. His skin had an unhealthy pallor, his nose, always a prominent feature, now stuck out like a beak, and his movements were slow, weary and careful. But it was his eyes that were particularly revealing. Once hooded and inscrutable, they were now fixed and enquiring, as if searching for something. An answer to a question they already knew. It was a long time since Jim had looked into such a pair of eyes, but at one time he had great experience of them. It was the stare of death.

'What I want to know is, when are we going to eat?' said The La imperiously. 'I've had coffee and buns with my little cavaliere servente —'

'Not even that,' put in Maurice pedantically, revealing that his cast of mind at least had not changed. 'You were never married.'

'All right then, my little would-be Cheri.' The La's expression was indignant, but she was immensely relieved. So was Jim. She pointed to him. 'He hasn't eaten for a week, his stomach is rumbling like an express train, so would mine be if my muscles weren't trained in the best Conservatori. And what have you had since lunch, my dear Rodrigo?' She often called Maurice this, because he reminded her of a baritone who had played with her in Don Carlo. She sometimes referred to Eddie and Maurice as Rodrigo and Carlo. It was the most she ever went in that particular direction.

'I'm not hungry,' he replied, walking slowly to the armchair by the fireplace and sitting down, gripping the arms with his fingers and stretching his long legs on the rug.

'That's beside the point. What I want to know is what's in the house? I have veal, but is there enough for us all?

36

You, I know, never have half a loaf when anybody wants anything.'

She stood up and clasped her hands over her bosom, making a big decision. 'We must all eat together tonight. I want to hear all about Europe. It has existed without me, I know, but how? You might well ask. And where will we eat? In my place or in Eddie's? You two savages have not even a dining table between you. Eddie's is the best, and I can do things on his cooker better than on my own. And the little pig always has loads of exotic things in his fridge.'

'Is he not home yet?' Maurice drew up his knees and covered them with his outspread hands. In his voice there was a querulous note, like an old man complaining of being alone. Jim looked down at the ground and frowned. Eddie should have been here.

For a moment none of them knew exactly what to say. The La, realizing that she had made a slip, went on talking about food.

But they had not to wait long. In the middle of a vivid description of how to make a real brodetto, The La stopped short and cocked her head. Not for nothing had she perfect pitch.

Eddie ran up the stairs and burst into the room, carrying a parcel which he dumped on the floor, shook Jim warmly by the hand, patted his shoulder and diffused such an air of welcome for himself and the others that Jim and Maria were more than willing to have themselves fooled by it. Only Maurice frowned and did not respond.

'We must have a fatted calf for the prodigal son. You will all come down to my place, and I'll cook it myself.'

'You can't cook for toffee,' declared The La, 'and you know it. Always buying expensive food which you stick in the ice-box and forget all about. You could open a delicatessen of your own if you weren't so lazy. I will cook the dinner and it will be good.'

She picked up her coat, gloves and bag, and laid hold of the parcel. But Eddie was too quick for her. He snatched it out of her hands and held it tight against his chest.

'I will carry this down for you while you are taking off

your Borgia ring and putting on your apron. We will all go down in a minute and get the place ready.'

As The La made her exit trailing clouds of Roman Hyacinth, Eddie turned to the others with a grin. He was sure of his ability to lighten the atmosphere once they had all got together. In some ways it was the most difficult task of all, and Maurice was the first to make that apparent.

'You've been drinking,' he said irritably. He knew that Eddie never drank to excess but it was a subject on which he was sensitive. Besides in spite of Jim's hearty greeting he had caught the look of alarm on his face when they first met. It had been instantly suppressed but it angered Maurice and he wanted to take it out on someone.

'As a matter of fact I was,' replied Eddie softly. 'And I intend to drink some more. We can't have a welcome home party without champagne, and I still have a few bottles of that from my birthday.'

'You've had enough,' muttered Maurice, struggling painfully to get out of the deep armchair. The others watched helplessly.

'All right, all right, I'll give it to The La. And Jim here looks as if he could do with something.'

'I could do with a bath.'

'Well then, have it. You'll be ready by the time we have things on the boil.'

Jim made a move towards the folding doors but Maurice, on his feet and swaying, was in a truculent mood.

'Why didn't you get home in time?' he demanded. 'You were not kept at the office. You never are. And you knew perfectly well that I had to go to the doctor.' He turned to Jim with the same expression, but lowered his voice. The other detected an appealing note and fumbled uneasily with the clasp of the partition. 'I've been having treatment with Isaacson across the way. Desmond sent me to him. I go there after the shop closes.'

'You couldn't go to a better man,' said Jim evenly. 'Has he got you on a diet or something? You've got thin.' It was a bold throw; but it succeeded. A welcome home is a welcome home, and even Maurice, much as he would have liked to destroy this evening, felt his anger ebbing. They were all doing their best, he knew that.

'I could do with a shave myself,' he said. 'I came back and had a bath at lunch time. You have to with these doctor fellas. I'll be ready before you.'

Jim nodded and passed through the doors, closing them behind him. Maurice and Eddie, left alone, looked at each other.

'How was it?' said Eddie gently.

'The same,' Maurice shrugged. 'What did you expect, a miracle?'

VI

The dinner party passed off fairly well, except for one revealing incident.

Eddie's flat on the ground floor was not quite as silent as Jim's. Beyond the drawn curtains one could hear the muffled purr of traffic, but it was easily drowned by the chatter of talk.

'Grace rang up,' said Jim as he came in, looking refreshed and soothed by his bath. He was wearing a light brown Italian sweater and pale grey slacks. Maurice was already down, sitting by the blazing coal fire, his silver hair neatly brushed and oiled. His haggard cheeks looked even more transparent and Jim thought it wiser not to mention that it was he who had done the ringing.

'How is she?' said Maurice.

'Fine. She and Desmond will be round today or the day after. Or sometime soon. You know the way they are.'

Maurice looked interested. He was fond of the pair and looked upon them with a certain amount of awe.

The La, who owed most to them, since they provided her with a rent free flat, took a haughty view of them, declared them philistines, and concealed her admiration for Grace, whom she considered a martyr. Desmond she could not abide.

Now she bustled in from the next room which Eddie used as a kitchen-dining room. Jim and Maurice had come to the conclusion that he had put it in for her, since she possessed only a gas-ring, and when not invited out to dinner would content herself with cocoa and toast, rather than forego the pleasure of Floris, a new scarf or another hunk of costume jewellery. But she was only allowed to use the kitchen when he was at home, for reasons which they all knew.

She was a superb, if somewhat slap-dash cook. Flushed, and wearing a tiny pink frilly apron, she stood fanning herself regally with a newspaper.

40

'Can I help you?' said Eddie anxiously. He was smoking his first cigarette of the evening, and Jim wondered if he was trying to give them up. It was the sort of thing he would do. If I gave them up Maurice would get better.

'Don't be silly,' snapped The La. 'But I could do with an aperitif. Mix me a very dry Martini.' While Eddie was preparing the drink Jim sat down opposite Maurice, who gave him a wry smile.

'The usual roses, I see,' said Jim. On a table between the windows stood a huge bunch of yellow roses. The La may not have been entirely correct when she declared that he smelled of them but he certainly had a passion for them. Maria had not been far wrong however. There was an element of symbolism in her identification of her friends' characters with certain smells. The roses represented a side of Eddie's nature, a voluptuous, sensual quality, of which he was more aware than anybody else. But he never used scent, for the simple reason that Maurice could not stand it, and often held his handkerchief to his nose when The La doused herself more recklessly than usual.

Eddie came and sat on the sofa on the side nearest to Jim. He launched into a discussion of the various cities which Jim had visited, talking with fluency and knowledge of all of them, but did not mention the nature of Jim's book until the end. It was a study of the present state of the Roman Catholic Church throughout Europe, the dissension within its ranks, the effect of the changes on the clergy and laity, weakening faith and the possibility of schisms and national churches in the various centres of Christendom.

'Nice to have a seven months tour of Europe paid for by the publishers,' he remarked, lighting another cigarette carefully.

'Yes, but I have to deliver the goods in three months time.'

'You've been making notes as you went along, haven't you? You should be able to put them together in that time.'

'I suppose so.'

'Miei cari, sedete,' cried The La, appearing without her apron and making a gracious gesture, 'e al convito che

41

s'apre ogni cor. In other words, you slobs, come and get it.'

They trooped into the hallway with its elaborate Georgian plasterwork and heavy mahogany doors, and passed under the fanlight into the room which Eddie had fitted up with a complicated German cooker he had never mastered. He had however a fine round dining table, now laid and lit with candles. They glowed softly also on the mantelpiece and in the window which looked out onto the long narrow garden. They began with Danish caviare, which Maria had rooted out from the depths of the fridge, followed by a superb Wiener Schnitzel for Jim, an omelette for Maurice, and two underdone steaks for herself and Eddie. Then cheese, and coffee as only she knew how to prepare it. Eddie drank one glass of champagne, Jim another, while The La finished the bottle by herself.

Jim's health was formally toasted, Maurice raising his tonic water to welcome him back. He was strangely moved, and felt a lump in his throat as he stared down at his plate. How long ago it seemed since he had come to this house, friendless, penniless and alone, to be given, when his shyness thawed, the same sort of welcome as prompted tonight's little feast. At that time he had been bewildered and bitter, having been politely told by two pious landladies that they were 'closing their rooms', after getting word of his past on the Irish grape-vine. No decent Irish landlady in 1967 was going to have her house polluted by a renegade priest. He remembered his appeal to Grace, her swift action, and his first confused weeks in, what seemed to him then, very luxurious surroundings. Only desperation could have prompted that call, for had not Grace in her own way been one of the unwitting causes of his defection? And now another cycle had come to an end. He looked up, caught Maurice's fixed, glassy stare, and forced himself to smile.

After dinner, replete with wine, The La made one of those gestures peculiar to artists, who can sometimes display the most blatant insensitivity under the impression that they are behaving with spontaneous generosity. Impulsive she certainly was, but she had also her full share of that ravening egotism without which she would not have been herself.

She got up, raised her chin and threw out her arms, wriggling her finger-tips in that time-honoured gesture of the prima donna 'milking' applause in Italian opera houses.

'And now, cari miei, I am going to give you a little extra pleasure.' She paused dramatically. 'I am going to sing for you. For you alone.'

They all looked up in surprise. Was the unheard of, the hoped for, the long since despaired of miracle about to take place? She cleared her throat and thumped her chest.

'I am not in good voice today,' she went on, and they all relaxed. The La had not been in good voice for thirty years, although they often heard her sing a phrase or two in her own room, which suggested that some notes were still intact.

'But I will play one of my records for you,' she declared grandly, sweeping to the door. 'And since I am putting it on myself, and it is my voice, it is exactly the same thing as a real performance. Eddie, I will use your radiogram, and leave the doors open, and none of you must stir.'

The La had a gramophone of her own, and often spent whole evenings listening to her own records. But Eddie had an even better collection, got together before he met her, and including the Irish songs which she effected to despise. She swept out, and they all sat back, expecting to hear the entrance of Butterfly, her favourite, or perhaps the love duet from Andrea Chenier with Pertile, which she modestly claimed was not too bad.

But with the first faint notes of the piano from the next room Eddie stiffened and sat up, clutching the stem of his glass, while he darted a quick worried glance at Maurice who was staring blankly in front of him.

The voice rose, distant and disembodied, as if it were coming from another world. It was one of the few recordings which Keeley had made in London in 1935, with Gerald Moore at the piano. Although she pretended to underrate these trifles, saying that they were purely commercial in the McCormack tradition, no one knew better than The La that 'Oft in the Stilly Night' was by far the best and truest recording of her voice in its prime.

It shimmered and glowed like a ruby, and the feeling and expression which she put into the words were a heart-felt cry from her own nostalgic Irish soul, and a tribute to the great accompanist, who succeeded in that session in making her forget the exaggerations of Italian opera, and refine her art, so that the simple little song became a universal lament for all things lost and fleeting.

As the voice swelled, luscious, impassioned and bright, yet strangely ghostly as it sounded from the other room, the three men avoided one another's eyes and sat rigidly still. The tangled threads of emotion, experience and sympathy which bound them together were stretched to breaking point. One moment of weakness, and the edifice which they had so carefully constructed over the years would have come tumbling down.

> When I remember all
> The friends, so linked together,
> I've seen around me fall
> Like leaves in wintry weather;
> I feel like one
> Who treads alone
> Some banquet-hall deserted –

They sat at the table by the light of the guttering candles as memories of the past swept through them with the terrible force which is the curse and the strength of the Irish character.

There was a long pause, carefully calculated on the part of The La, before she made her reappearance. It gave the men time to recover themselves somewhat. Nevertheless when she made her entrance, she was taken aback by the silence that greeted her. And then Maurice shambled to his feet, and inclined his head towards her. The others immediately sprang up and applauded, after which Eddie said he was going to play some of her opera recordings and hurried from the room.

The La sat down, smiling graciously and a little sadly.

44

After all, she too had had her past, and not much of a future. She toyed with her coffee spoon and looked into the distance, as her voice rose triumphantly over the orchestra in the rapturous phrases of the duet from the first act of Madame Butterfly.

Ah! quanti occhi fissi, attenti! quanti sguardi!

Perhaps her earlier gesture, although it was not devoid of conceit, came from some secret corner of her heart, one wiser than she knew. She had faith in her little circle of friends. If the suave tune, the hackneyed words of the Moore melody caused them to break down, the actress in her might have been flattered, but she would also have been dismayed. She had unwittingly tightened the screw, and it had not given way.

VII

'Well, May, how is the world treating you?'

'All right. Why don't you lock your car?'

'Do you think anybody would rob it outside your father's door? Besides there's nothing in it.'

Eddie put the keys into the pocket of his overcoat, and smiled at the girl leaning over the gate of the tiny front garden. She did not respond, but looked down the road with its line of identical cement houses, towards the corner. Her face was preoccupied, even anxious.

'Waiting for Daddy?' Eddie knew well that she was. The first time he called at the house three years before she had been in the same position, and she had asked him the same question about the car. But not since. It had taken time to get through to her, making it a great moment for him when she hopped up and down, clapped her hands and opened the gate when she saw him arrive. That had been a full six months after their first meeting, and it had taken almost as long with the others. Eddie was not good with children. They made him shy and a little scared but gradually he won them over, and counted it one of the triumphs of his life when the whole brood, with the exception of the baby, crowded about him one evening in the hall, pulled at his coat, tugged his trousers, and shouted at the tops of their voices, until they were driven away by their mother.

'Is your Mammy at home?' he asked, a little anxiously. It seemed to him that he noticed a change in the children in the last few months. They were more silent, less boisterous than they had been. And May in particular.

'She's upstairs,' the girl motioned with her head, and opened the gate in what seemed to him a grudging sort of way. He had heard of the frightening intuition of children, and felt alarmed at this change.

May turned back and walked the few steps to the door,

where the key was in the lock. She pushed it in, shouted 'Mammy', then turned round to go back to her station at the gate: an awkward, plain-faced girl, with lank straight hair and the serious, almost harried expression that one sometimes sees in the eldest child of a large family. She was eleven, the first of six who followed in rapid succession. Three other girls, and then the two little boys, made up the Hughes's brood. But May was her father's favourite; and Eddie's also. He realized that behind the shyness and awkwardness, perhaps because of them, there was something unusual in the gawky girl. She had a strange poetic mind, and was already an omniverous reader. Eddie had given her a set of Jane Austen and was delighted with her response. And recently he found her reading 'Wuthering Heights' in a way which made him wonder. She could not possibly understand such a book, but some strange current in it touched her imagination and transformed her plain face as she looked up from it. He remembered feeling the same thing as a boy, and suddenly felt very close to May.

But were they beginning to get sick of him, he wondered, as he stood in the tiny hall-way, staring at the childrens' coats hung up on the rack, and inhaling the smell of gas-cooked fried bread and sausages which emanated in waves from the kitchen. In spite of May's call Dolly made no appearance. Two of the girls, Florrie and Tessie, next in age to May, and as pretty and cuddly as she was plain and intense, peered into the passage, and came forward hand in hand to greet him. Their brown curls were tangled, and they both had jam smears on their chins. They pursed up their mouths and giggled but it seemed to him that they were a lot less playful than they had once been.

'Hullo,' he said, laying a hand on both heads, 'have you been good girls today?'

They looked at each other solemnly, and Florrie extended a grimy hand which he shook gravely, and held out his other to Tessie. She had always been the merriest of the lot, and after a moment's hesitation, flung herself upon him and hung onto his sleeve, tugging at it petulantly.

'All right, all right,' he said soothingly, 'I have them, but

47

not till Mammy comes. They have to be divided.' He always came primed with sweets. Blackmail at the beginning but later on, he liked to think, no more welcome than himself.

'Mammy is upstairs,' said Florrie, jerking her thumb in that direction, while Tessie repeated the information. The two little girls exchanged a glance and drew together again, looking up at him with round fathomless eyes. Women, he decided, began their mysteries early.

Then just as he was about to take the sweets out to pass the time, there was a flurry on the stairs, and Dolly came running down, contriving to smile at him and frown at the children at the same time. Mysteries indeed.

'Go back into the kitchen and finish your tea. You have Mr Doyle destroyed with your jammy hands. Look at his lovely coat.' The little girls clasped hands, scurried along the passage and disappeared.

'Take off your coat,' said Dolly, stretching out her hands for it. 'I'll give it a dab of parazone before you leave. They have your sleeve ruined. Isn't it well for you that hasn't a houseful of screaming brats up to God knows what at all hours of the day.'

Eddie smiled happily. The fact that she had just such a houseful was one of Dolly's chief attractions for him, although he was genuinely fond of her for herself. She was one of those small dainty women who manage to keep their figure in spite of constant child-bearing. She hardly came up to Greg's shoulder, and was a head smaller than Eddie: a blue-eyed, brown-haired little creature with quick nervous movements, and a warm lingering smile.

As she took his coat he was enveloped in a strong odour of eau-de-cologne, and noticed that she had smudged her mouth with lipstick, and primped her hair. Hence the delay.

'Come in, come in,' she said, opening the door of the small front parlour, in which a fire was already burning. Television in the corner, a picture of the Sacred Heart over the door, a small hard, three-piece suite and a glass china cabinet. Here Greg liked to relax, read the paper, and watch television when he was at home.

'Not back yet,' Eddie put down the bag of sweets on a small table beside a geranium in a brass vase.

Dolly sighed and shook her head. Her eyes had faded a little, her hair lost its lustre, and her forehead was furrowed. She had a habit of raising her eyebrows and opening her eyes wide. Eddie once told her to stop it or she would have her forehead all wrinkled but she asked him what on earth did it matter now. It was a subject on which he would have liked to lecture her but he could see that it was useless. And yet she must take some care of herself. Dressed to go out she was still as neat and pink as a Dresden doll. Now however, she sighed and gazed through the window.

'I never know when he's going to be home now. Leave cancelled every other week, with all those marches, and they never seem to have enough men. Poor Greg comes in for more than his share. If he was only as cute as some of the others and knew how to play his cards. Oh they're a right pack, some of the Guards, I can tell you.' Eddie smiled at the pun, but Dolly was unaware of it.

'I wish they were all as nice as him,' he said without a trace of embarrassment. Greg treated him like a big stolid brother dealing with a clever but not altogether understandable younger relative, in spite of the fact that Eddie was several years older. A hint of condescension on both sides helped to preserve the balance between them.

'That's what's wrong with him, he's too nice. If he was only up to the tricks of some of the others, he might have got promotion by now. Ah sure, what's the use of talking.'

'May is out at the gate, waiting for him.' The subject of Greg's promotion was one they had discussed at length before.

'God help her, the poor child, but she dotes on that man.' Dolly's eyes grew misty. 'And he on her. I don't come into the picture at all.' She sat down and held out her thin blue veined hands to the fire. Tiny claws, they showed the ravages of hours of washing and scrubbing. Eddie took out his cigarettes and offered her one. After a ritual hesitation

49

she accepted, and they both lit up. Dolly drew in smoke greedily, and exhaled it slowly and luxuriously through her nose.

'She's got brains, that one,' he went on, not inhaling. Jim had been right: he was trying to give them up – a pathetic votive offering. Dolly's greedy enjoyment of her cigarette made him think of Maurice, and his face clouded for a moment.

'Too much, maybe. She can see through you. I don't know where she got it, not from me anyway. But there's brains on Greg's side. Look at how that brother of his got on in the Income Tax. Ah, but sure you know him.'

Eddie nodded. Greg came from the same part of the midlands as himself. They had discovered when they met that their families knew one another well after the country fashion. But he was not thinking of that now.

'I hope to God she doesn't see through me,' he said with a sad smile. Not that he ever felt that he was deliberately concealing anything in this house. He was a friend of the family. Greg certainly was no fool, in spite of the lack of ambition which eternally delayed his promotion. He enjoyed the conversations and arguments he had with Eddie. It was not the sort of company he would normally get and it made a welcome change in his dreary round of duties. And their native place was a strong bond between them. They spent a lot of time talking about the large country town where Eddie's brother carried on the family business, and Greg's parents still lived on their farm a few miles outside. Nevertheless there were certain aspects of his life which Eddie would never have dreamed of discussing here.

Now Dolly looked at him with her round blue eyes; and it seemed to him that they were a little glazed.

'Ah, sure, what is there to see in you,' she said, unaware that she was paying him a great compliment. 'Isn't she always talking about you and the lovely books you give her? That's the way of her. She's no good at making up to people. Talk about seeing through people. I'm the one she sees through.'

50

She finished her cigarette, and to cover his surprise Eddie produced another, which she accepted without her usual reserve, lit it from the butt of the first and inhaled deeply.

'I suppose she doesn't think I'm up to much here.' She tapped her forehead. 'But she's all for her daddy. Look at her out there now, will you.' She coughed hackingly and Eddie concluded that she was smoking too much. He did not blame her. It was no joke dragging up six children and there were no luxuries in the Hughes' home, except for a telephone which was kept mostly for emergency messages. Indeed he had often wondered why the house was so shabby in these days of HP. He could only suppose that poor Dolly was not as good a manager as some.

'Has your friend come back?' she asked timidly. 'Mr Dillingham.'

'Oh, yes, three days ago. He's back into his routine. Doing a lot of writing.'

'Isn't it well for him to be able to go off like that, all over the world. And then to be able to write a book about it. It's a great gift surely.' She dragged on her cigarette and frowned with a kind of awe. 'And Mr O'Connell?' Her voice was still more timid. She knew about Maurice's illness, whereas Eddie was sure Greg had not told her about Jim's former occupation. She leaned forward with concern, and Eddie did his best to assure her.

In fact Maurice had seemed better for the past few days, which was why Eddie had driven out to Dalkey to see the Hugheses. He was now living very much from day to day. When Maurice had a good period, Eddie found hope still rising in his heart. Perhaps that way he could pass on some of his own health to his friend.

'Thanks be to God. Sure, I never believed he was as bad as you said. I knew a man was given up thirty years ago, and he's still in it, having seen half of his family down. But you must be famished after your journey out here. Would you like a little drop of sherry?'

She got up, drew the curtains, and went to the china cabinet, where the visitors' bottle was kept, and took out two glasses.

51

'Do you know,' she said as she handed Eddie his dose of the vile stuff, 'I think I'll have a drop myself. I have a cold coming on, and it's murder in this house with all the children.' She poured herself a glass, and tossed it back like water. Eddie thought that it was easy to see the poor creature didn't know how to drink. She took it like medicine. She put her glass back in the cabinet, and began to puff with quick nervous breaths.

'Are you cutting down on the cigarettes?' she asked suddenly.

'Well, I'm trying to.'

'Aren't you great.' There was a note of genuine envy in her voice. 'I can't give them up. Nerves, I suppose. Ah, sure I'm no good for anything. I wish to God I was a man like you. You have the life of Reilly, and know how to make the most of it. Ah, yes indeed, it's well for you.'

Eddie was surprised. But before he could think about it, there was a shout at the gate, and Dolly jumped to her feet.

'That's himself. But he won't be here for another five minutes. Would you believe it, but May knows if he's on the bus and it's coming up Ulverton Road. I'm telling you, that one has second sight. She even knows the days he'll be kept on duty, because sometimes he leaves a message and they forget to ring. If she's not at the gate, I know he won't be home, telephone or no telephone.'

VIII

And so it turned out. It was nearly ten minutes before Greg
came into the room, holding May by the hand. Time for the
bus to climb up the steep turn at the bottom of the road,
and let him out at the corner of Dalkey village. It took him
about four minutes to walk home from there, up Barnhill
Road and into the new housing estate. May could only see
him when he turned into their road. The little girl was
transformed by the arrival of her father and Eddie was
struck once again by the sweetness of the smile that lit up
her heavy features. It was then that she showed her
resemblance to her father.

'Well, well,' he said in his midland burr, 'and how is the
prodigal son? I bought a packet of sweets for my Mamie,
but I can see you have made a show of me again. She won't
have much welcome for this now.' He produced a small
paper-bag and handed it to the child. He always called her
Mamie, the only one who did.

'Oh, no, Daddy,' cried May loyally, clutching the bag.
Then she caught Eddie's eye, dropped her eyes and shuffled
her feet with embarrassment.

'That's a nice thing to say to Mr Doyle,' said Dolly,
frowning. May gave her a quick, searching glance, and
Dolly drew in her breath sharply.

'It *is* a nice thing to say.' Eddie was touched by the
child's candour and passionate devotion to her father. He
took it for granted that she was equally fond of her mother
but she saw her all day, every day, except for school hours,
whereas her father often spent days and nights away from
home.

'It is *not*,' insisted Dolly crossly. 'Now, go in and set the
table for your father's tea. And not one sweet out of Mr
Doyle's present will you get, if I have anything to do with it.
Go on now, miss.'

'I don't want them,' flashed back May, as she hurried

from the room. Dolly, looking flustered, stared after her, muttering something about having a genius in the family.

Eddie found the little scene both touching and funny but neither Greg nor Dolly seemed to think so. His face hardened as he unbuttoned his belt, took off his jacket, and lowered his huge frame with a sigh into the armchair opposite Eddie.

'Well, did you ever hear the like of that!' exclaimed Dolly.

'Aw, can't you leave the kid alone,' muttered Greg, loosening his tie and puffing out his lips.

'That's all right for you,' snapped Dolly, 'you don't have to ...' Then she remembered her guest, gave a rueful little smile, and shrugged prettily. But he knew she was annoyed. 'I'll get a cup of coffee for you later,' she said. 'I know that's what you like.'

When she was gone, Greg looked down at the sherry glass which Eddie had placed on the floor beside his chair. The hectic red roses on the carpet had faded with the years, to their distinct advantage.

'A slow drinker, I see. You're a wise man.' Greg ran his hand through his thick brown hair and turned down the corners of his mouth. His shirt was too tight for him, and he ran a finger round the inside of his collar, pulling at it with relief.

'I have a few bottles of stout in the car ...' Eddie began eagerly, knowing how Greg liked his couple of pints in the evening. But to his surprise the big man shook his head and looked stern, wearing his professional expression, which made a curious contrast with his loosened collar and the lazy way in which he had been scratching his chest.

'No, Eddie. I'm trying to give it up.' He patted his stomach. 'Have to watch the weight.'

To judge by his wedding photograph Greg Hughes as a young man had possessed features of almost mathematical regularity; something which Eddie noticed was one of the distinguishing marks of those who followed his profession. Had it something to do with a mind and body completely equipped by nature to follow without questioning the dictates and morals of the majority of society? Now at thirty-six, his handsome face had harshened and his figure had thickened, but he had not run to seed. He had only a slight paunch, and kept himself in trim by swimming at the Forty Foot as often as he could. He moved with a slow bovine tread but Eddie knew that he was still remarkably agile on his feet, and gave the impression sometimes of being ready to spring like a big cat. The La said that he smelled of lions and had a feline eye. Eddie had been much impressed afterwards to discover that Greg was born at the end of July.

'If you had been at home today around four you'd have had to do your duty,' said Greg with a smile, as if he had read his thoughts.

'My God, not again!' Eddie threw back his head and looked at the ceiling. 'Where was it this time?'

'Louis Wine, the antique shop. She made off with a silver jug, worth four hundred pounds, or so Wine said.'

'Who retrieved it?' He took up his glass and fortified himself with a sip of the poisonous sherry.

'Mr Dillingham.' Greg always paused before the 'Mr.', which Dolly never did, thus proving that the yellow-eyed policeman could be discreet even in his own home. 'The usual ploy. He just went into her flat, asked her to get something for him out of her bedroom, picked up the jug and handed it out to me. And that was that.'

'Will I ever forget the time she kept that porcelain vase of mine for three days and insisted that it was hers. Do you know when we managed to get our hands on it, she threatened to report it to you?'

'Ah, well,' said Greg philosophically, 'that's the way it goes.' This expressed succinctly the attitude of all those who knew of The La's weakness. Madame Maria Keeley, Ireland's pride and joy, the idol of every singing teacher and pupil in the country, suffered from a mild but curious form of kleptomania. A constant visitor to the best antique shops in Dublin, she was in the habit of picking up some piece which appealed to her and walking out without paying for it. At the beginning the dealer concerned had thought it was a slip of memory and had been much alarmed when she returned his bill in a rage, declaring that she had never bought anything from him in her life. Mr Wine, for it was he, had not pressed the case. No one wanted to bring the darling of Erin into court for shoplifting. But the word had gone round.

Desmond had been contacted – it was before his marriage – and a plot was hatched between the then occupants of the flats. The antiques were to be collected from The La the moment she arrived home, for it had been discovered on the second occasion on which she had been found lifting, that Madame Keeley did not seem to mind in the least if the object was retrieved immediately, and gave no sign of missing it.

This was first discovered by Mr Dooley of Dawson Street, who knew the couple living in the flat before Jim arrived – a retired colonel of the Indian Army and his wife. The colonel had taken swift action. He snatched the silver snuff-box from the table in the hall where The La had nonchantly deposited it and hurried back to the shop. Thereafter a plan had been agreed between the antique dealers of Dublin. They welcomed the great lady as before, but kept a weather eye open for anything missing after she had gone. If anything was, a Guard was immediately dispatched to call on Colonel Fetherstonhaugh who entered into the spirit of the thing with great enthusiasm, and invented a hundred strategems to gain entry into The La's flat whenever she took her booty that far, lay hands on it and return it to the waiting policeman.

But the good officer and his lady – who thoroughly disapproved of the whole thing, and regarded The La as an immoral woman on the strength of an outrageous story the singer had told her of her relations with Mussolini – had long since departed for happier hunting grounds. When Eddie moved in, the position had been carefully explained to him by Desmond, and it was in this way that he met Greg Hughes who was often on the beat in Grafton Street and its purlieus, to which exclusive neighbourhood the prima donna confined her activities.

When Jim moved in the main action of the plot fell on him, since he was in the house most afternoons. The operation was fairly easy since The La never attempted to conceal her treasure and more often than not, just left it on the hall table. If she brought it down to her flat Jim had to think of something he wanted out of her bedroom, while he hi-jacked the stolen goods back to the front door. On one occasion he had returned to receive a powder puff, the only thing he could think of at the time.

'I'm surprised at you,' The La said archly. 'Bringing ladies to your apartment. Are you sure you don't want anything else, a few safety pins, perhaps?'

It was a typical Irish compromise, in which face was saved, and a hell of a good time was had by all. As the years went by it became an institution. The La would boast about all the kind, young policemen who were forever escorting her home, for in time she got to know most of the men on duty. And if she saw one of them following her, she would slow down and walk back with him herself. In this way she caused more than one shy young rookie to blush all the way from Grafton Street to Fitzwilliam Square. But eventually she succeeded in charming them all, and a signed photograph of the prima donna hung in the parlour of many a mother who had given her son to the cause of law and order in Ireland.

'All the same,' said Eddie, suppressing a smile, 'it's a good thing she doesn't go in for it in a big way. The antique dealers know her, but supposing she took to lifting stuff wholesale from the big stores.'

'Oh, well, then she'd have to be put in St John of Gods.' Suddenly Greg sat up, and gripped the arm of his chair with whitened knuckles, his tawny eyes blazing. The implications of the statement seemed to have hit him after he had made it. 'Christ God, Eddie, wouldn't that be fucking awful!'

Eddie was surprised by the force of this outburst. There was no doubt about it, The La had a way with her. He nodded in agreement.

'It's odd though how she claims it belongs to her if she

can keep it a day or two. She said my vase had been given to her by some Italian prince.'

'What's this about an Italian prince?' said Dolly, coming back with a tray of coffee and biscuits. 'Is it Miss Keeley ye're talking about? They played a record of hers on the wireless yesterday, "Oft in the Stilly Night", and do you know what, the tears were streaming down my face when it was over. She must have had an awful glamorous life. I've read about it often, but just think what it must be to be hearing it all from her own lips. Greg, your tea is ready.'

Dolly watched him leave with bright anxious eyes, patting her hair nervously. She chatted to Eddie for a few minutes, looked at herself in the mirror, and shook her head.

'I'm a sight again after frying. Would you mind if I ran upstairs and powdered my nose?'

'Of course not.' Eddie chuckled and settled in for the evening. Greg would come back – the children would be brought in one by one for their treat. The youngest girl, Bride, already an accomplished flirt at four, would climb on his knee and make eyes at him. The little boy, named after his father but called Sonny, would stare solemnly and try to snatch as many sweets as he could from his sisters, while the baby, Eddie, who was his god-child, would be carried in either sleeping or bawling, before going to bed. Then Dolly would dart in and out, while he and Greg talked about home. There was much to discuss this evening; six deaths of well known neighbours in the last fortnight. He lifted his cup and put it down again half-way to his lips. In his enjoyment of this unfamiliar atmosphere in which he was so cheerfully accepted as a sort of honorary uncle, he had for the moment forgotten about Maurice. No, they would not talk about those funerals this time.

Dolly came hurrying back, and perched herself on the sofa. More eau-de-cologne. Eddie was almost overpowered by the scent. And she had applied so much powder to her face that she looked like a clown, while she had smudged her mouth with lipstick, and had clearly forgotten to do anything with her hair. The whole thing was a bit overdone, he thought, feeling pleased by all this artless primping.

'Do you know what,' she said, looking at him with her saucer eyes, 'I'd give anything to meet her, Miss Keeley, I mean. Only I'd be ashamed of my life. I wouldn't know what way to look, or what to say. But ...' She bit her lip, and the smudge got worse.

'Well, why on earth don't you?' he exclaimed. 'There's nothing The La adores more than an admirer. Come in any evening, and I'll introduce you. She'll give you a signed photograph.'

'Oh, do you think she would? I could show it to my mother. Only I wouldn't like her to think I was pushing myself. Greg would be mad. Maybe, you won't tell him.'

'That's a deal, Dolly. I won't tell him. But I'll fix it up with The La. She'll be thrilled.' Eddie smiled at this harmless illusion about the glamour surrounding the poor old La. If Dolly only knew. Dolly, happily married, with her healthy brood, her decent, quiet husband and her hum-drum life, which might seem ordinary to her, but was far from so to Eddie. It never occurred to him that either of the Hugheses had illusions about him. In fact both of them – although Greg had some private reservations – were convinced that he led a wonderful, carefree, exciting life. No money worries, no family ties, hordes of witty and glittering friends and in spite of all, not a bit of side to him. Equally it never crossed Eddie's mind that he harboured a fair amount of illusions about the Hugheses himself.

Presently Greg came back, patting his stomach, and looking very serious as he always did after a meal. Dolly got up to see about the children and Eddie sipped his coffee which was out of a tin and tasted like ink.

'Do you think that Dolly looks a bit edgy?' said Greg suddenly, in a low voice.

'Well, now that you mention it, a bit maybe. I'd get her a tonic or something. It's no joke coping with a family these days. I'm a great believer in raw eggs myself, but you'd have to get them up from the country. The battery eggs they have in the shops here have no food value at all.' Eddie spoke as if he were an authority on life and the nourishment of overwrought mothers.

'I'll write to my mother about it,' Greg frowned and rubbed his forehead. Eddie thought how lucky they were with their small everyday worries.

Suddenly Greg changed the conversation. He began to talk in an indignant tone about the curse-of-God nuisance all those damned marchers and demonstrators were making of themselves. Greg did not like blacks, saw communists everywhere and insisted that the RUC in the north were a much maligned lot. With none of this did Eddie agree and they had a spirited argument, which was broken only by the entry of Dolly and the children. And in spite of everything they ended up talking about the deaths at home.

For an hour or two Eddie forgot his worries and it was nearly eleven before he got away, parting from Dolly with a conspiratorial wink.

'Ah, it's well for you,' she sighed. It was something he was to remember.

IX

Maurice sat in the old armchair in his bedroom, looked at his wrist watch, and slowly clenched and unclenched his fists. The La was out to dinner, Jim was working on his notes, and Eddie had not yet returned. It was exactly ten forty-seven. He held the watch with its thick leather strap against his ear and felt a strange sensation of comfort, as the minutes ticked on relentlessly. Here at least one knew where one was: time neatly and effectively divided into minutes, hours, days.

But when he took his hand away and let it fall on the arm of his chair, he immediately experienced a return of that sense of drowning, of being carried along on a deep, slow tide and sinking under it, which he had more than once become aware of recently whenever he was alone.

The room was absolutely silent. As he always woke up at exactly the same time each morning, even in his drinking days, he had never bought himself an alarm clock and to have one as an ornament would never have occurred to him. The fat tick-tock of a time-piece above a blazing fireplace, accompanied by the contented purring of a cat, and the bird-like chirrup of a cricket on the hearth were not sounds that appealed to him. He remembered that from his boyhood, when he had preferred to hide himself in the loft, or go on long solitary walks over the fields rather than join the circle round the fire. How often had he come back, drenched to the skin, in time to join the last decade of the rosary and to meet his mother's reproachful glance as she got up stiffly from her knees. There had never been any comfort for him at that fire and, as time went on, he avoided it more and more. His harsh early upbringing had done its work. It was designed to fit him for a life that was narrow, hard and fatalistic. He preserved those elements in his nature in an even more inflexible form when he left home, filled with vague but savage dissatisfaction with the way of life in which he had been reared. An old story. He could not have remained anyhow. There were two brothers older than he, and there was barely enough on the farm to keep the old people.

But in his case the reaction against his upbringing was made more violent by the discovery of something strange and alien in his nature; something for which the code he inherited made no provision.

He stood up and began to walk slowly about the flat. He had never bothered to furnish the front room, since he never entertained. It was carpetless and empty, except for a table in the corner piled with books. All his possessions were contained in the back room where he slept. Some coloured prints of places he had visited abroad with Eddie hung on the walls, but there were no souvenirs, no ornaments. A bed, a table, a couple of armchairs and a record player beside a pile of records in the corner were all that the room contained, apart from a few suits in the wardrobe and his linen in a chest of drawers. It was not particularly tidy but it was scrupulously clean, and The La had not been without justification when she claimed that he smelled of leather. Being in the business, he had more shoes than he needed. They were ranged in a make-shift rack under the window and, since some of them were brand new, there was always a faint scent of leather in the room.

He stopped and looked at his watch again. Time, freed of its arbitrary segments of minutes and hours, became a vast amorphous tide. The moment he thought of the second, of the smallest unit of time, it was gone, to be succeeded by another and then another. The present, when one tries to grasp it, does not seem to exist at all, except in theory. It can only be understood by the ticking of minutes. The past and the future had some sort of shape and validity and for him there was now little future. He could not shape it in his imagination, as others did. This new sense of the meaninglessness of the present, without clocks, appointments and the hum-drum activities of the daily round, produced a sense of terror. He felt beads of sweat gathering on his forehead and upper lip and a clammy film enveloped his body. He raised his wrist to his ear, and pressed the watch against it.

62

X

He was so preoccupied with the tiny sounds, so intent on keeping himself afloat, that he did not hear the quick steps on the stairs, or the door opening. Eddie rushed in.

'Maurice, are you all right?' The voice was quick and breathless, and it brought him back to life. He relaxed, sat down leaned back and nodded.

'Why, what did you expect?'

'I didn't realize it was so late. And the traffic was awful.' In earlier times Eddie had often come back to find Maurice sitting alone like this, staring into space. Then he would have made a joke of it, asked him what the nightmare was. But now such questions were impossible. He was reduced to wariness and trivialities, and hated it.

Maurice held his watch up to his ear again instead of looking at it, a gesture which confused Eddie further. What did this mean?

'I know that,' said Maurice in a voice too gentle and calm to be natural. It sounded as if it came from far away. Eddie was frightened, and turned aside to take off his coat. He knew it was impossible for him to conceal anything from the other's piercing gaze. It was part of the mysterious affinity between them, transcending the physical attraction about which both of them had always been cautious, exercising a control upon it which had not always been easy. As a result the understanding between them became more acute: but there were times recently when Eddie wished that it were less so. He dreaded showing the anguish he felt.

He sat down and clasped his hands. Since Maurice first told him bluntly of his condition they had avoided any serious discussion of it. Eddie was so stunned that he had been unable to think of anything to say, and since then had strained every nerve to keep up appearances, hoping against hope that the whole thing would prove to be a false alarm. Even in his thoughts he fell back upon cliches. But he did not tell Maurice that he had gone secretly to Clarendon Street and given in money for masses to be said. In moments of crisis Eddie always reverted to the religion he had ceased to practice for many years and still clung to in his bones.

'I suppose you've been telling the holy Hugheses about me, and asking them to offer up the Rosary,' said Maurice with a sarcastic smile.

'I've been doing no such thing. I told them you had not been well, and were getting better.'

'Another lie. But then that's what keeps you going in that set-up. Lies. I don't know how you stick it. All those whining brats, and the little woman coping with a brave smile, I bet, while the man of the house hums and haws for fear he'd say anything contrary to the Constitution. A bloody polisman.' Whenever he was annoyed Maurice's Roscommon accent came out strong. 'Don't you know that the only good cop is a dead one? Trying to get all he can out of you. I bet you have to pay your way for the privilege of sitting with the elect. Christ Almighty.' He hardly raised his voice or moved a limb. Since his illness he seemed to be conserving his strength. The rough voice, the barely controlled savagery with which he once would have uttered such opinions were now lacking. And this new quietness was even more intimidating.

Eddie made no reply. They had been through all this before. The first time he visited the Hugheses, Maurice had given him a long searching look on his return. Any suspicions he had that Hughes represented anything really dangerous for his friend were immediately dispelled.

'I won't go any more,' said Eddie simply. 'But there's no harm in them. In their own way they find things just as difficult as we do.'

'You don't have to stay away because of me,' grumbled Maurice, feeling more irritated than ever. 'It doesn't matter a damn anyhow, one way or the other.'

'That's quite right, it doesn't.'

'Then what are you yapping for? To hell with the

64

Hughes and all the rest of them.'

Eddie got up and looked around the barely furnished room. It was here that Maurice had hit him on the mouth, drawing blood, the first time he had made a tentative, ill-judged approach to intimacy. Here too, after many weeks of tense mutual trial, they had come together shyly and clumsily in what most of the world thought of as an unnatural and unmentionable love.

'All right Maurice, you've had it out on me.'

'Forget it,' said Maurice, running his hand over his thin face. Eddie took the opportunity to light a cigarette with trembling fingers. His fifth that evening. Ordinarily he smoked ten or twelve after supper. He sat down again and crossed his legs, feeling the pulse behind his knee racing.

'I know how you feel.' Maurice clasped his hands and pressed them against his chest. 'We're eejits to be talking like this. It isn't as if I was thinking much of that now. It's a bit late in the day. What I'm wondering about is how long I'll be able to go on working.' He lifted his thin shoulders as if he felt a sudden chill.

Eddie had often tried to think what he would say when this moment arrived – and always ended by putting it out of his mind. But now he felt curiously calm.

'Did Issacson say something?' He grasped his wrist to steady the hand which held the cigarette. His inner numbness did not extend to his fingers.

'No. But some day soon, he's going to tell me to lie up. I might have to go into hospital. And there's the expense. The insurance will cover things when it's all over. But I haven't that much saved, about three hundred in the bank, as you know. God knows how long this damn thing will last.'

'You won't be going into any hospital,' said Eddie firmly. 'You'll stay here.'

'Oh.' Maurice raised his thick eyebrows. 'Have you been discussing this between you?'

'No,' declared Eddie, knowing well that that lie would not pass. 'You'll stay here. I'll look after you. You see I've never been as pessimistic about this as you.'

'My bitch of a sister-in-law bunged my auld father into the country-home when he began to wet the bed. The poor auld bastard never knew what hit him.' Maurice made an attempt to smile, baring his strong white teeth but Eddie knew he was not angry. 'Of course you've discussed it, you and The La and Grace. And the fellow below.' He unclasped his hands and jerked his thumb at the floor, looking at Eddie narrowly. 'Have you noticed any change in him?'

'No, why?' Eddie thought he had; and knew what was coming.

'I'd say he isn't such a renegade priest as he pretends, especially since he came back from this tour. Not that he ever was, in my opinion. And I know what Grace and The La have in their heads. And you too, when it comes to the bit. It would make you all feel more comfortable if you got me fixed up in the end. This brings out a lot of hidden things in people, and I have a feeling that it'll bring them out in Dillingham more than anybody.'

'Yes, I *have* noticed a change in Jim.' Eddie tried to avoid a direct answer. 'He doesn't seem too happy about his new book.'

'Fuck his new book,' snarled Maurice. He got to his feet slowly, swayed for an instant, then recovered himself. 'But I want you to promise me that you'll let me leave this world in my own way. And you know what that means.'

Eddie crushed out his cigarette on an ash-tray near his elbow. He scattered sparks on the carpet and stamped on them with his toe. Then he raised his head and met that dark, implacable stare.

'I know.'

'And you mustn't ever regret it. They'll try to make you. I know them. But if you're thinking of accepting them, ever, you'll have to reject me now, and everything that has happened between us. Otherwise, even that has been a sham. Well?'

'I'll never deny that, Maurice. You needn't be afraid.'

There was a silence during which Eddie felt that the other man was trying to search his very soul. It was not the first time that Maurice had frightened him, but he had

66

never felt so completely helpless before.

'I don't care much for the idea of pain, I needn't tell you. But they've got drugs now, haven't they? I don't want immortality and all that shit. I don't believe in it, and I never believed in it less than I do now.' He paused and slowly held out his hand. Eddie looked at it blindly, then held out his and felt it grasped in a hot dry grip that fastened round his fingers like a rope. 'You'll do for that,' the deep voice went on. 'So long as you live, I'll live. That's the only kind of survival I'm interested in.'

On Maurice's wrist Eddie could hear the large watch ticking. It was all he was aware of at that moment of committal.

XI

'Would you believe it, but this house was bought by Uncle Walter in 1912 for four hundred pounds, and he thought he was robbed.' Desmond raised himself on his toes, gave a quick glance of approval in the mirror and smiled with satisfaction. 'Just think what property is going for now.'

'Do you remember him, Jim? Uncle Walter, I mean.' Grace made a face as her husband preened himself.

'No, that was before my time. He had been home a year before I came and died shortly afterwards. I'm sure I remember that. I came the year after.'

'He was a great-uncle, as you know,' went on Grace, looking at Eddie, who was putting drinks on a tray so that Desmond could pour his own and look after the rest, something he loved doing, even when not in his own house.

'I remember him well.' Eddie put down the tray on the table beside the bowl of roses and straightened up, his strained face brightening a little. 'Your grandfather's brother. I remember your grandfather too, although he died in '45, I think. Shocking, isn't it, that I can look that far back. He was the image of your Aunt Anne. She was much more like him than her own father.'

'They were quite different,' said Desmond, going to the tray and pausing to consider what they would all have. Whiskey for himself, sherry for Grace, and a Martini for The La when she came in. Jim was already provided for; he and Eddie had been drinking gin-and-tonic before the guests came in. Maurice, sitting silently by the fire, was drinking nothing. 'Uncle Walter was the go-getter of the family. Lucky for me that he was. What a haul he'd make now with all this speculation.' He laughed, a high explosive hoot, as he poured out the drinks and prepared to hand them around.

'I hope you're not thinking of putting this house on the market,' said Eddie anxiously, catching Maurice's brooding eye. 'We'd all be out on our ears.'

'He is not,' said Grace firmly, taking her glass and looking at her husband with a slight frown.

'Of course not,' said Desmond easily, as he carried round the tray, going about his task neatly, gracefully and with complete assurance. A small, well proportioned man with sharp regular features, he walked briskly with a peculiar stiff-legged gait.

'How is Dick?' went on Grace, looking at Eddie. 'Have you heard from him recently?'

'Yes, indeed.' Eddie squared his shoulders and thrust forward his head aggressively in a fairly accurate imitation of his brother's stance. It was his first party gesture of the evening, and an awkward one. 'The usual. Trade Unions, government controls, rates going sky high. Plenty to grumble about. I'm kept going with the millers. Oh, by the way, he told me those new people who bought your house are turning it into a hotel. I suppose you've heard.'

'Good God, no, I haven't!' Grace's face dropped, and her mouth opened in dismay. 'How dreadful!' Involuntarily she looked at Jim, who shook his head and smiled sadly.

'I remember passing it once,' said Maurice suddenly. 'On the bus going home. Somebody told me it was the Condon house. I couldn't see it of course, only the gate lodge and the trees. The fella beside me told me there was an avenue half a mile long up to the house.'

'Nothing like that,' smiled Grace. But it was clear that she was upset by the news.

'All the same, it seems a pity,' went on Maurice dourly. 'I usen't to go home that way usually, but that time I missed the other bus and had to go round by your way. Little did I think I'd meet you all like this. Eddie's house was a little farther along the road, and I was told it had an avenue nearly as long.'

Grace looked affectionately at Maurice. She had always felt drawn to this strange man and was glad that he seemed to accept her as a friend.

'Oh, our house was nothing like Condon's,' said Eddie. He was about to say that at least his brother was still in occupation, but stopped himself just in time.

'It's a good thing your Aunt Anne doesn't know about this,' said Jim quietly. 'She'd turn in her grave.'

Grace and Eddie looked at him in surprise, while Desmond turned from the mirror, where he had been giving himself another admiring glance, and raised one eyebrow with delicate affectation. Then remembering his duties as host, Eddie changed the conversation and they began to talk of trivialities.

A stranger overhearing the conversation which had gone on before would have been puzzled. It was very much like the private jargon in which some families indulge. And indeed the ties between Grace, Eddie, Desmond and Jim were complex and deep-rooted. Eddie and Grace were perhaps the closest to each other in many ways. They were the same age, had played together as children. Their people had known one another for four generations. They were bound by memories of births, deaths, marriages and the subtle rivalry of two families of equal importance to themselves. The Condons were richer and had made more important connections in England and Ireland. The Doyles were a little older in the provincial hierarchy of establishment, but had remained closer to the ground and perhaps, as a result, had survived longer in their native place. Eddie's brother had three sons to carry on his name and business.

Grace and Desmond were first cousins and their marriage had given rise to much unfavourable comment. His mother had been the favourite niece of the great-uncle Walter they had been speaking about. He had settled in Dublin, gone into contracting, built and bought a great number of houses, invested shrewdly and died unmarried, a very rich man. His niece married an Anglo-Irish squireen, Raymond Fitzgerald, who was related to some minor English nobility. Their son Desmond inherited all his mother's property, which she had shrewdly kept from the clutches of her shiftless husband.

Grace also was an only child. Her mother died in giving her birth, and her father followed his wife ten years after. The family business, a large wholesale hardware and timber-mill, was managed by her unmarried Aunt Anne Condon who had taken the place of a mother. She had been an admirable woman, strict and hard-headed in business dealings but generous, warm-hearted and completely devoted to her niece, who adored her. She died of cancer when Grace was twenty-five and when she knew that her illness was fatal, advised the girl very wisely to accept an offer from a big combine for the sale of the business. Grace was left with a considerable fortune, a big house which she did not know what to do with and little idea of what she wanted to make of her life. She was desolate.

At that time Jim Dillingham had been a young curate in their parish. He attended the aunt during her last illness and afterwards took an interest in the handsome, gentle-mannered girl, which ripened on his side – during a period of doubt and confusion – into what he was convinced was love. Grace herself was but dimly aware of his feelings, which he was too shy to declare, and when shortly afterwards Desmond arrived on the scene, he sized up the situation and, one memorable evening, put the priest's emotions into a few, short revealing words and drove him in a panic from the house. This experience, combined with the trouble he had got into by the publication of a book which he had written under a pseudonym, made him leave the Church.

Shortly afterwards, Grace, lonely, confused and miserable, married her first cousin, sold her house and went to live in Dublin. The tide of the years had swept them all together again, and the ties of the past were still strong, although Jim had long ago realized that he had never been really in love with Grace. She was part of his protest, but he remained extremely fond of her.

'You know,' said Desmond, standing with his back to the fire and gesturing with his glass, 'You're all a bunch of provincials. I'm the only one who was born here. And the whole lot of you in your hearts really hate this gorgeous old whore of a town. Fusty indeed! A lot Dublin cares what you think.' They had been discussing The La's description of

71

Dublin as smelling like an empty theatre during rehearsals. Fust and canvas and cats, she had declared, that's what it smelled of.

'She isn't far wrong,' said Maurice unexpectedly. 'I can see what she means. But I always think of gas. Every digs I stayed in, before I came here, they had gas cooking. I never got used to it.'

'For me ...' began Grace and Eddie at the same time. They stopped and looked at each other knowingly.

'Coffee?' inquired Grace softly, and Eddie nodded.

'The chocolate factory at Islandbridge,' he explained. 'The first thing you smelt as you were coming into Dublin from the west. Grace and I came up to our first pantomimes together. Jimmy O'Dea used to be in the Olympia in those days, and Ivy Tresmond at the Gaiety.'

'Not very gallant,' murmured Desmond, lifting his eyebrow. It was always the left one.

'My martini, please,' said The La, appearing at the door. She was in her best velvet, for this was the first time the Fitzgeralds had come to supper since Jim returned. They had dropped in to welcome him back on their way to the theatre a week before, but tonight was special. The La had been busy with a huge spread of risotto and veal cutlets cooked in the Milanese fashion which would have done credit to Biffi's. Desmond handed her her drink and she beckoned to Grace.

'You know, you get more and more like Flagstad every day,' she said as Grace rose and joined her, smiling a little anxiously. It was clear that The La wanted a little private chat.

'Very complimentary, I must say,' laughed Desmond, who was an inch shorter than his wife, and very conscious of it.

'Don't be silly,' snapped The La. 'I'm talking about her face. Kirsten was about twenty stone heavier than Grace and six feet taller. But the face, o dio mio, so like. The same nose and eyes and chin.' She patted Grace affectionately on the cheek, took her by the hand and led her out.

'Flagstad, my God!' Desmond raised himself on his toes

72

and lifted his chin. 'She looked like a tank.'

'Oh, no,' protested Eddie. 'She was very beautiful, and The La is right. Grace really does look like a younger, slighter edition. It's quite a compliment in other ways too. The La knew Flagstad in Vienna and she's the only soprano I ever heard her say a good word of. Not the same repertoire of course.'

'I hope she'll be able to come to Bridget Porter's dinner party, next week. The La, I mean. Even Bridget can't conjure up a ghost.' Desmond reverted to his favourite topic, for he was a dedicated if harmless snob. 'There's going to be a mixed bag, a pop singer from England who lives on hash and chips, a few of the tweeds to hurry on their apoplexy, and that new writer who's got himself banned. The La will slay them all. You know how Bridget adores her.'

Jim and Eddie exchanged glances and smiled politely. There was no stopping Desmond when he got onto this sort of thing. Maurice was the only one who showed interest. It was part of the illusion he had about the Fitzgeralds and one of his inconsistencies that he always displayed curiosity about the Porters. Lady Bridget, after several marriages, had reverted to her family name which was the subject of innumerable Dublin puns, since her enormous fortune was founded on beer. To be entertained by her was the ambition of every social climber in the country. She was as dumb as she was beautiful but Desmond, whose father had known her as a deb, insisted that she was a fountain of wit.

He prattled on and Maurice listened to him intently. His grey face gave a curious impression of youth, now that the lines had been erased by the shrinking and stretching of the skin; an illusion heightened by the child-like pleasure he derived from hearing about the doings of these shallow and glittering people. Eddie who had heard all this before and knew the Porters only too well, was glad of the interlude. Desmond was good for at least a quarter of an hour of this and Eddie had a shrewd suspicion that Grace had not been called into the other room to help with the cooking. Presently, he excused himself and slipped out.

73

XII

'I want you to talk to Eddie.' The La tucked the white coat which she used for serious cooking under her chin, folded the arms and quickly rolled it up. She held the bundle for a moment against her breast, and looked at the door.

'Don't worry about that, child.' The La shoved the house-coat into a cupboard and waved her jewelled hand at the oven. 'It'll keep for a few minutes. Besides your little boy will be telling them all about his social triumphs. Misericordia, what a baby he is, cara! Jasus, Mary and Joseph, so are they all, all men, bambini! How they talk. We're safe until their bellies begin to rumble.'

Grace sat down at the candle-lit table. The room was warm and comfortable, the polished table with its white mats gleaming like a dark lily pond in the soft light. She looked up at her friend.

'What do you want me to say to Eddie?'

Maria did not reply directly. She twisted her emerald thoughtfully for a moment and squeezed her eyes shut, as if she were flinching from an unpleasant thought.

'They know nothing,' she said in a low voice, opening her eyes and rolling them to indicate the next room where Desmond's high-pitched laughter could be heard. 'Nothing about the things that really matter.' By this she meant births, deaths and marriages which, like all women of her generation, she considered the exclusive domain of her sex. The fact that she herself had never married, and that Grace was childless also, did not shake this conviction in the least.

'They have courage,' said Grace quietly, picking up a fork and tapping it against her wrist. 'Eddie and Maurice, and Jim too. They're not finding that talk very easy. It covers up a lot of things.'

'What do you expect them to do? Roar crying?' The La made an impatient gesture and a blue-green flame darted from her ring. 'What is life but putting a face on things? We all do that. Yes, they have courage. I know, I know, ah, crude sorte. But that's not what I mean.' She sat down

74

opposite Grace, pushed one of her candle-sticks aside and leaned her elbows on the table. 'Do you think our little Eddie is religious? You know what I mean.'

'I know. I think he is.'

'But of course. I can see it here.' Maria put up her fingers in a V to her forehead and drew them down to her nose. 'And the stubborn priest, the one who thought he wanted you but will never love any woman. He has it too and can settle his own accounts. Oh, I know that none of them go to Mass, but what of that? Men are like that, it means nothing.' She shrugged her shoulders and shook her head with Latin wisdom. 'But the other one, Maurizio.' She clasped her hands tightly. 'O, my dear, you must speak to Eddie about him. We have spoken of it between us before, Eddie and I, but now, no more. Something has happened, and I am frightened for him. For both of them. You see, with the sick one it is different. With Eddie and the priest it is here, in the head. And that's not so bad. But with the other –' she thumped her chest and stomach – 'It is in the heart and the guts. It is something very dark. I have seen it before, not often, but it is terrible. He is like a man who could kill himself, not just physically, in the body. It is much worse than that, so I am afraid for both of them, and that is why I want you to speak with Eddie.'

Grace was sitting with her back to the door, and saw the old woman's face change. It tautened and a mischievous twinkle came into her eyes.

'And now tell me, how has your little boy been behaving? Boasting of his conquests? As if you cared. That spoiled brat was never in love with anybody but himself.'

Eddie had just come in. The La's change of expression was swift and brilliant, but her conversational ploy had not been so successful. Besides Eddie heard her last few words before she changed the subject.

Grace turned and looked at him. She had noticed earlier the change in him since their last meeting. She expected him to become livelier, even arrogant in company as time went on. That, she knew, was his particular form of courage. But tonight he appeared withdrawn and preoccupied, and his eyes were veiled and uneasy. It was not the usual patient reserve he displayed when Desmond was holding the floor.

It was clear to her that he knew what they had been talking about. But this was neither the time nor place for intimacies. She fell back, as shy people so often do in moments of emotion, on her social manner.

'We were talking about you,' she said calmly, with that slight frown he remembered from long ago, when she was cautioning him in the presence of elders. 'It's ages since you've been out to see us. Come next week for tea. Surely you can get away from your sinecure for one afternoon.'

It was not an invitation, but a command. Eddie understood perfectly. He would be back by the evening and Maurice would be none the wiser. Besides he wanted to go.

'Yes, it has been a long time. I could do with a breath of country air.'

'Tuesday?'

'Yes, I think I can manage that.' It was clear that Grace wanted Desmond out of the way.

The La rose majestically and flashed her emerald.

'And now you can tell them that supper is ready. It'll be spoiled. We thought you men would never stop talking. Yap, yap, yap. Has Desmond got round to Bridget Porter's third husband yet? The one who told her he liked his dog better than her? Perhaps he was right.'

XIII

The Fitzgeralds lived in Leixlip, in a 17th-century house, one of the few of its kind still in use round Dublin with three therme windows on the third floor. The front door opened on to the village street but there was a large garden running down to the Liffey behind, where the salmon weir was now covered by a concrete layer put up by the ESB.

Eddie always enjoyed his trips to Leixlip, apart from the pleasure of seeing Grace. How often had he passed the place on his way to and from Dublin in the old days. It was on the road home. Topping the hills outside the pretty little village, with its row of quaint Huguenots' houses, his father used to say that he could get the first wind from the west. Years afterwards, Eddie remembered this when he saw the painting by Jack Yeats of the Dublin quays with a side-car facing Kingsbridge, entitled, 'A Westerly Wind'. These two memories, his father sniffing the breeze beyond Leixlip and the vivid evocation of the simple scene by the Liffey, had mingled in his mind, producing an impression of poetic nostalgia – half-dream, half-reality – to which his nature responded with a sort of child-like rapture. It seemed to him entirely appropriate that his oldest friend, a woman who was in so many ways a pivot in his life, should be associated with these gentle and powerful images.

When she was expecting him she always opened the door as soon as his car drew up outside.

'Desmond has run into town,' she said as he took off his coat in the hall and threw it over a chair. 'He might be back before you go.'

'What have you sent him in for?'

They smiled, but Grace did not reply as she slipped her arm through his and drew him into the drawing room which, like all the rooms in the house, was richly alive.

'You'll have a drink before tea,' she said, 'and so will I.'

While she was busy at the tray, Eddie sat down by the fire and looked about him, not noticing anything in particular. He was one of those people who absorbed

77

atmosphere but could never remember colours. He formed a vivid and sometimes clairvoyant impression of people and places, often amazingly accurate: especially of strangers with whom he could take an objective view, but he had little interest in taking notes. Besides, he knew this room as well as his own.

Desmond, like many people who have little to do and no particular talent for anything, was a dab hand at interior decoration. His house was much admired, full of rare period pieces, exquisite carpets, solid hand-carved silver and dark Jacobean chests and tables. Yet the effect was one of spaciousness and light, achieved by a cunning placement of mirrors and glasses opposite the windows. There was no feeling of design, self-consciously created, partly due to Desmond's cleverness but mostly, in Eddie's opinion, because of Grace's calm and natural absorption of her surroundings.

Grace handed him his gin and tonic, sat down in the high winged chair opposite with the glass of sherry into which she had poured a few drops to keep him company.

'Any change?' said Grace, who always came to the point at once.

Eddie shook his head and sipped his drink. The clock in the hall struck four.

'He has his good days, of course, and there are times when one would think he was almost himself again.' He looked up with a sudden gleam of hope. 'Did you notice anything the other night?'

'Not really.' Grace, having tasted her sherry, left it down on the table beside her, folded her hands and looked into the fire. 'He was always quiet, one of those people I feel I don't have to make conversation with.' Then she looked round the room, as if to indicate that she often found it necessary to do exactly that with many of the people Desmond entertained. It was an unusually quick movement for her.

'He was always very fond of you. He has romantic notions about you and Desmond.'

Grace smiled.

'Which means that he doesn't really want to know us all that well,' she said, a little sadly. 'There are so many things one thinks about and wants to do at a time like this. All the usual things, one does that. But somehow it never seems enough.' By this, Eddie understood that she wanted to do something more – and knew that she was not the one to do it.

'There are some people like that,' she went on thoughtfully. 'One likes them and feels that they respond, and you are more conscious of it when they're difficult, and don't seem to need so many of the things that the rest of us do. I don't think that I've ever really known him, certainly not the way I know you, and now I wish very much that I did.'

'No one could have done more than you've done,' said Eddie haltingly, bringing out each word separately. He had the sensation of playing for time.

'Jim knows him. I've always felt that. In some ways they're curiously alike.' She leaned her cheek on her hand and looked at Eddie with that diffident but steady expression which he knew so well. It meant that she had something serious on her mind, and was not going to allow anything to deflect her.

'You think so?' he said lamely.

'Well, they're both solitaries. They're both natural ascetics at heart. I don't suppose many people would say that of them, but how many people understand anything below the surface?' She smoothed her skirt, as if she were brushing off crumbs – a habit she had – while Eddie reflected that it was not necessary to delve into the unconscious (an area of which he was suspicious) to arrive at that conclusion about Jim and Maurice. 'I don't suppose they have ever been very close, have they?'

'No.' Eddie frowned thoughtfully, a little disturbed at the turn the conversation had taken. It made him uneasy since he felt that they were touching upon something very close and mysterious; in which he himself was involved. He sensed what it was, but felt that he would never dare formulate it. 'After all, there was always me,' he went on with an attempt at playfulness.

'I don't mean that.' She made a slight gesture of dismissal and Eddie began to feel uneasy.

'I don't know what would have happened to Maurice if he had not met you.' She clasped her hands and leaned forward. 'Jim, I think, would have survived more or less as we know him now. But in their time both of them have been betrayed. Maurice has not become reconciled.'

'And Jim has?' There was an edge on Eddie's voice. He felt on the defence.

'I don't know. Perhaps not to what he was, but I think he has come to terms with himself.'

'You mean he's no longer in love with you.' Eddie's voice was still sharp. He had a confused feeling that he was defending Maurice; something he had never felt the need to do before with Grace.

'He never was.' She shook her head. 'You know that as well as I do. He thought he was.' She chuckled softly. 'I was someone to talk to and, of course I needed somebody too. After Aunt Annie died. And then there was that awful business with Father Geraghty. Even I didn't know about the book at the time, but Jim had to tell somebody. Authors are like that, I suppose. It must have been terrible for him to discover that his closest friend had ratted on him.'

There was no need for Grace to go into details of this affair. Eddie remembered it well. Father Geraghty had been a class-mate of Jim's at Maynooth. Unable to keep the secret entirely to himself, Jim confided the news that it was he who had written 'Faith without Guilt' to the man he thought of as his friend. But Geraghty was also attached to the palace and he was ambitious; he was jealous; he was disturbed by the theme of the book which seemed to him, as it did to many other clerics and laymen at the time, heretical. A mixture of all these motives inspired him to inform the bishop who censured Jim firmly, but with a certain sympathy. He insisted however that the book be examined by the diocesan censor, who gave as his opinion that if it had been submitted it would never have received the imprimatur. The book must be sent to the

80

Holy Office in Rome. Knowing the fate that awaited it there, Father Dillingham refused to submit it and left the Church. No publicity attended his departure. He simply dropped out and was left to sink or swim on his own. The bishop, Dr Curley, was the man whose retirement he had read of the day he got back.

'Geraghty died last year, didn't he?' said Eddie, looking at the carpet.

'Yes, just before Christmas. Shortly before he wrote to Jim. He told me about it but not what was in the letter. But I sense a change in him since, especially since his return from abroad. Did he speak to you about it?'

'About the letter? No, this is the first I've heard about it.' He shrugged and not for the first time that day remembered his promise to Maurice. He had never kept anything from Grace except the physical details of his affairs. What were they all trying to do? And would he in the end be able to bear the burden of another man's soul?

'Why should he?' he said lightly. 'It has nothing to do with me.'

'Hasn't it?' said Grace quietly.

'Jim doesn't seem to think so.'

'But perhaps you do.'

And of course she was right. He did feel it was something that touched him, just exactly how or why he could not have said. But there was a key here somewhere and he experienced a moment of cold panic as he realized that it led to a door he was forbidden to open. He took up his glass and drained it, coughed, took out his handkerchief and blew his nose.

'Why all this talk about Jim?' he countered, his voice deepening with nerves. 'He's well able to take care of himself.'

'I should think we all are by this time.' Grace turned away and looked across the room. It was long past tea-time. Grace had evidently given word that she would ring. 'I've noticed of recent years that everything is beginning to be a twice told tale. Desmond and I, you and Maurice, Jim and the Church, all our memories of the old days, The La. It's all happened before, and none of us are much wiser. There's only one thing that matters when you get to my age and that's acceptance. The exact same thing as my grandmother used to tell me.'

'It depends very much on what you accept,' said Eddie.

'Some people never accept themselves, Eddie. They try to live through others. I suppose they can't be blamed, but it can't be done, not ever.'

'Don't we all? We all live through others, you, I, all of us.' He knew what she was trying to get at, whether she really understood it or not.

'In a way,' replied Grace, without a hint of uneasiness. 'But there are limits; a certain line beyond which no one can go.' She paused. 'It's the sort of thing Jim could explain better than I.'

'Naturally, he's a priest. Scratch him, and you'll find all the same old answers.'

'If you find that, after all he's been through, then it might be worth listening to. At least it won't be bland. I don't know any new answers to anything myself, and I doubt if he does either.' She stood up, her tall majestic figure outlined against the bronze November light framed in the window behind her – the high straight forehead and the Grecian nose thrown into sharp relief. In all the years he had known her, Eddie had never ceased to wonder at the classical beauty of this profile, all the more unexpected since Grace's full face was broad and very Irish, with its high cheek bones and small soft eyes.

Tea was on its way. Grace hurried to the door and opened it, to admit Bridget (the other Lady, Desmond called her) holding a heavy silver tray. She welcomed Eddie with a friendly nod, shook hands with him when she had put down her burden and chatted for a few minutes. The old house-keeper had come with Grace from her Aunt Anne and knew Eddie since he was born. For her nothing had changed and Henry Doyle's son could do no wrong.

'Two lumps?' said Grace.

XIV

'Desmond,' said Grace presently. A few moments afterwards there was a sound from the hall – Desmond's homing call, a sort of owl-like hoot, part of their private language – and he bounced into the room, rubbing his hands and chanting:

'Go little duck, and wish to all
Flowers in the garden, and meat in the hall.'

He often made such entrances. Unlike most people, who like to be thought better read than they really are, Desmond took a peculiar pleasure in impressing upon others the fact that he had never read a book in his life; which was not strictly true. When therefore, he picked up some jingle or some resounding phrase, he delighted in misquoting it over and over again. It was one of his shock tactics.

Grace laughed as he kissed her cheek and shook hands with Eddie, giving him a comically wicked leer.

'Tea. Tea for the master, and make it strong.'

Grace looked up with a curious expression in her eyes, half-anxious, half-indulgent which Eddie had often noticed before, whenever she was listening to her husband. Desmond, having made his entry, settled himself on the sofa, crossed his legs and twiddled his thumbs on his flat stomach with a benign, almost sleepy expression on his face.

He chattered away as Grace poured out his tea; a slow, easy conversation which was kept up while the 'master' tucked in with the happy eagerness of a boy just home from school.

It was no news to Eddie that Desmond was quite a different man in his own house. The self-conscious poseur, with his tiresome little snobberies and brittle mannerisms, who liked to give the impression that he was a cynical man-of-the-world, was revealed here as a rather spoiled child; a boy-husband – in spite of his forty years – who was very much dependent on his wife, had complete faith in her judgment and thoroughly enjoyed being mothered by her. So do we all, thought Eddie, who knew of the harmless little affairs which Desmond had had since his marriage. These, no one took seriously, least of all the women involved. They had all discovered that Desmond was one of those born flirts who, like all true narcissists, are essentially timid and lacking in passion. It was not necessary for him to 'go back' to Grace after one of those exercises in vanity: he had never been away.

In this, Eddie − whose acute instinct was sometimes dulled by self-deception in his relations with those who possessed all the conventional qualities he lacked himself − was dead accurate.

Grace Condon was one of those women, more common than is generally supposed, who have a strong maternal instinct, without any great urge to engage in the intimacies by which it can be fulfilled. She loved children, but wished very much that nature had devised some other way of producing them. Instinctively she was drawn towards men whose masculinity was somewhat uncertain, or so much under control that she felt free from restraint in their company. Eddie had always regarded her as a kind of touchstone. She had an uncanny intuition which never failed to divine sexual aggression in men, overt or repressed. Once Eddie in his younger days had introduced her to a willowy youth, with undulating hips, limp wrists and the mannerisms of a music-hall female impersonator. 'I would not,' she commented quietly, 'like to be stranded on a desert island with that man.' And sure enough, he turned out to be an indefatigable womaniser, now long married, divorced, remarried and the father of six legitimate children in all.

With Desmond, the tie of blood had been a great help in overcoming her natural timidity. But even here she had chosen a husband who was less a mate than a naughty if affectionate little boy. Eddie supposed that in the beginning they had lived together as man and wife, since Grace's idea of a woman's part was essentially Victorian, and her longing for children genuine. But they had remained

84

childless. Perhaps her psychological dread of the sexual act was too deep-rooted to overcome her passionate desire for a family. Eddie knew from Desmond, who had no understanding of this side of his wife's nature, that she had consulted several doctors, all of whom told her there was no reason why she should not become a mother. In the end, like all of them, she accepted her fate, and filled the empty space in her heart by adopting a little family of her own that she watched over with a jealous and tolerant eye, finding some compensation in their obvious devotion to her. It was this asexual, maternal quality which appealed to Maurice, allowing him to indulge one of the few illusions he permitted himself. To him the Fitzgerald's life seemed remote from the sordid brutality he saw all about him. But Eddie was well aware of the sadness that enveloped them, in spite of their gay comradeship, financial security and full social life. And he had a shrewd suspicion that Jim realized it also.

'I must dash,' Eddie said. 'It'll take half-an-hour back with the traffic coming out.'

'Oh no,' protested Desmond energetically. 'Stay to dinner. I thought you had meant to.'

'He has to go back,' said Grace quickly.

'Oh well.' Desmond got to his feet reluctantly and turned his back to the fire with his hands held out behind him.

Eddie paused for a moment before crossing to the big window that overlooked the garden. There was a fiery sunset which turned the withering leaves that still clung to the beeches at the end of the lawn to purple. Putrefaction: the dying of the year. A clump of Michaelmas daisies reared their mauve heads against the brick wall, itself the colour of dried blood. Nearer, peony-flowered dahlias still bloomed, a muted blend of white and yellow, while a line of border chrysanthemums slashed the fading green of the grass with crimson bronze.

He was peculiarly sensitive to the onset of winter and watched the fall of every leaf with jealous care. They had not switched on the lights while they were talking by the fire, and now the room seemed to reflect the melancholy of the pall-bearing colours outside and the sense of sadness which had descended upon them.

The battlements of the castle across the river, owned by cousins of Bridget Porter, were black against the lurid sky. Eddie felt tired and vaguely frightened. He had always been fascinated by the thought that under all the brittle rose leaves, the wilting hedges and the dying trees showing their skeletal bones, the seeds of another spring were slumbering under the black earth. Now, for the first time in his life, he feared this re-awakening, feeling underneath his weariness and sorrow a mysterious stirring of something inexorable and unknown. It was like sensing the beginning of a growth in the depths of his being which he did not want to think about, like a man who suspects the existence of a tumour that is feeding upon his substance. He felt his body grow cold and his heart beat faster as he stood watching for what seemed a blurred segment of eternity. The dusky colours suddenly dimmed before his eyes and he pressed his hand against his forehead. It was burning. The moment passed, and the realization came to him with exquisite probing clarity that it was not death he feared, but life. The spring would come again into this tranquil garden, predictable and familiar. But what would come of the emptiness he felt within himself?

It was time to go.

Part Two

I

Maurice, walking very slowly along the sunken path outside the park railings, felt something brush against the top of his hat. He put up his hand with a great effort and grasped the overhanging branch of one of the trees which was lower than he ever remembered before. It would have to be loped and Maurice was not sorry since, like all Irishmen of small farming stock, he hated trees. They were suitable only for ornamental purposes where no potatoes flourished, and were the exclusive concern of the ascendancy with their high walled demesnes. He could never tell one tree from another, no matter how often Eddie told him. 'You and your bloody trees,' he would mutter scornfully. 'A lot of good they are to anybody!'

He stopped and grasped the branch. It was covered with small black buds, or so it seemed to him. On closer inspection, he discovered that their colour was dark brown; the shade of a Franciscan habit. He scratched the terminal bud with his fingernail. Underneath was another coating, lighter in colour, like the bay pony they had for the trap at home long ago. He dug his nail viciously into this and encountered the soft white pulpy kernel from which later, in the spring or early summer as Eddie could have told him, the delicate feathery leaves of the ash would unfold. He let go of the branch and walked on, remembering that it was the first of February, a Thursday that year. St Brigid's day. In the old days his mother would walk the three miles to the chapel with her half-dozen 65% wax candles to be in good time for the blessing next day. Before she went, she always hung the St Brigid's cross outside the door, over the snowdrops, just as on May Day she would strew the threshold with primroses.

As he reached the corner of the small park, he glanced down the street. It was a high soft-winded day – a foretaste of spring – and the sharp sunlight danced and gleamed on the white plaster frames of the long line of windows leading down to Baggot Street. Reflections of the sinking sun rippled like yellow velvet up and down the tall shallow-looking houses out of which at that hour the office workers, the doctors' receptionists and the government commuters, were hurrying to parked cars and bus-stops. Caught here and there by a glancing beam, even the granite fronts of some of the area basements glittered. A big brown Mercedes was turning out of the garage at the bottom of Fitzwilliam Place where Eddie kept his car, and Maurice watched it dully as he waited to cross the street. A woman in furs, a man in an overcoat with a velvet collar were in the front, while a spectacular fawn Great Dane was lying in the back. For some reason the sight irritated him and he glared at the small hurrying woman who bumped into him at the bottom of his own steps.

He ran his hand according to habit along the polished brass rail inside the front door. Eddie had told him that in the days when families entertained in these houses, the railings had been put up to preserve the walls from the shoulders of last-minute loungers. The La said they always reminded her of the bars at the ballet-school in Milan, and claimed that it was her unfulfilled ambition to stand on her toes with the door open someday, and lift her leg as high as she could.

Eddie's door was ajar and he looked up from the book he was reading as Maurice came in. In two months he too had lost weight and, although pale and wan, looked younger and more alert than he had been for several years. His clothes needed letting in but he kept putting it off, so there were times when he looked like a young man wearing his father's suit.

'Did you meet Dolly going out?' He no longer asked Maurice if he had had a good day. He could tell by his movements as he took off his coat and threw his hat over it that this was one of them. But his bad days were now a great deal worse and he had remained in bed over Christmas; a festival he particularly detested.

'Oh, that one. So that's what she looks like.'

Maurice sat down, trying to recollect the blurred face of the small, shabbily dressed woman he had bumped into.

For some reason he had been left with an impression of big frightened eyes.

'She's always in a hurry.' Eddie nodded towards the door. 'I caught a glimpse of her running out. I thought she'd drop in and you might meet her.'

'What would I want to meet her for?' Maurice wiped his upper lip with his forefinger and realized that both were sticky. He thought of the gluey bud with distaste, got out his handkerchief and wiped his hand carefully.

Eddie said nothing. After much hesitation, Dolly at last made her first call on The La on New Year's Eve. Since then she had been in several times, always in the afternoon, so that Maurice had never met her. Although The La pronounced her to be a sweet little thing, and gave her the promised signed photograph and Dolly was breathless in her praise, Eddie got the impression that she was scared stiff of her idol. Yet she continued to come.

A last shaft of sunlight flickered through the window and lingered for a moment on a table beside Maurice's chair. He could feel the faint warmth on the back of his neck and was conscious of something glimmering on the table. It was a gold snuff-box with a miniature of a young man on the lid. More often than not Eddie kept it locked in a cabinet but he sometimes took it out, especially when the Fitzgeralds were coming. They had been in the night before to congratulate Eddie on his first appearance in print and Desmond again made an offer for it. Grace, who knew perfectly well that it was not for sale, was amused at her husband's conviction that a long, subtle and clever bargaining game was in progress and kept putting up his price a little every time he saw it.

'Is that another book you're reviewing?' Maurice looked at the thick volume on the arm of Eddie's chair. It had a highly coloured dust-jacket.

'Well, I suppose I will. They seemed to like the first piece. Besides, they're short of reviewers and Jim hasn't the time.'

The literary editor of one of the Irish dailies had the same publisher as Jim, knew of his trip abroad and asked him to review some travel books. Jim asked Eddie to try his hand, being well acquainted with his fine critical sense, and feeling that the work would help take his mind off other things. His first article had appeared on the literary page the previous Saturday in company with several well-known names. Maurice, who possessed in full measure the old Irish awe of the written word, was much impressed, and Eddie, who was secretly proud of his first effort, had agreed to do it regularly.

'It's only hack work. Reviewing is the lowest form of animal life. I'm just filling in space.'

'You might as well get paid for it. You'd read anyway. And free books too. What does that one cost?'

'Twelve pounds. It's really only a coffee-table book by one of those pushing peers who cash in on their names. Desmond knows him and of course thinks he's the cat's whiskers. In fact he has the mind of a money-lender. Which is just what's needed for this sort of book. I'm going to pan it. Not that it makes any difference what I say. He's got all the gossip columnists behind him.'

'It's a right racket. And another fifteen quid for writing about it. I'd say you're on to a good thing.' Maurice did not make it clear whether he thought the book or the review belonged to the 'right racket' and Eddie was opening his mouth to defend himself when The La swept in, switching on the light to make her entrance more effective.

'Where is that child?' she demanded, looking about the room, as if she expected to find Dolly concealed behind one of the chairs. 'She told me she'd drop in to see you before she went.'

'Dolly? She must have changed her mind. Maurice met her on the steps. I expect she discovered it was later than she thought.' Eddie stood up and tucked the book under his arm. He had left the review slip on Jim's desk and could not remember the date of publication. Besides, it made a handy book-marker.

'What would you like for your tea, Maurice?' he said as he went to the windows to draw the curtains. Since Christmas Maurice no longer went upstairs when he came back from work. He and Eddie ate together and the sick man remained in the flat until it was time to go to bed. In those long evenings, during which they listened to records or sat and read, both were aware of a closer sense of communication than ever before. They did not talk much; it was not necessary. Maurice, in spite of his growing weakness, seemed in a curious way happier and more serene. He spoke even of the Hugheses once or twice in a distant, half-humorous tone. It was only when Eddie attempted to talk about themselves that a flash of his old harshness returned.

'Don't worry,' said The La. 'I'll get it.' It was a ritual question, since Maurice no longer ate anything for supper except tea and toast.

'I must wash my hands,' he said when Eddie had gone out, struggling slowly to his feet.

'What did you think of her?' The La gave him a curious look and lowered her voice. 'The little Hughes creature, I mean.'

'I hardly noticed her. She bumped into me at the bottom of the steps. I didn't know who she was.'

'Pity. I'd like to know what you think of her.'

'Why?' Maurice raised his eyebrows in surprise.

'She smells of berries, Rodrigo mio. Juniper berries. You know what they make out of them?'

'What?' Maurice's voice was careless as he walked to the door, his mind intent upon soap and water.

'Gin, my dear boy, Gin!' Her voice rose with rich dramatic effect. 'Santo Dio, what fools men are. They never notice anything. The woman was sloshed, pie-eyed, d'you hear me. I noticed it the first time she came, but now I'm sure.'

'Probably took one too many to give her the courage to face you.' said Maurice sardonically. But he remembered those wide frightened eyes, and immediately dismissed the thought. The world was narrowing.

'Nonsense. She doesn't come to see me. It's …' she broke off and shook her head. He was gone. She was just about to follow him into the kitchen when she saw the snuff-box on the table. She clasped her bosom and took a deep breath. A sly, greedy, longing expression clouded her eyes. For a moment she looked like a fat child eyeing a pot of jam. She lifted her head, listened intently for a moment, then darted across the room with light springy steps, snatched up the box and thrust it into the cleavage of her velvet dress. She was out of the room and down the stairs to her own flat in less than a minute. She ran into her bedroom, thrust the gold box under her pillow, patted her chest and returned at a leisurely pace, humming softly to herself and greeting Eddie with a gay smile as he came downstairs with the review slip in his hand.

'I want to talk to you about Dolly, Carlo mio. Oh, the poverina, I think you should know.'

'Know what?' Eddie was already thinking of the first sentence of his review.

'Later, bimbo. First we must eat.'

II

That evening Jim Dillingham had an unexpected visitor.

The door bell rang in his room. At first he thought someone calling on one of the others had pressed the wrong bell, and continued typing. During the last month the book had begun to flow and take shape since he decided to write for himself and disregard the formula which he knew the publishers were expecting. He hoped to have the first draft ready in about six weeks, being one of those men who, when possessed by an idea, write with great rapidity and desperate intensity lest he impede the development of his argument.

The bell rang again.

He stood up and hurried to the door. It occurred to him that one of the editors who had lately been pestering him for articles and reviews might have called, and Jim whose livelihood depended on his books, could not ignore the game of literary politics; much as he detested it.

He opened the door just as the person outside was turning away, reaching out a hand to grasp one of the spikes of the railing to help him descend the steps.

'Yes,' said Jim politely. 'Were you looking for me?'

The stranger turned and the light from the hall fell full on his face. The same face that Jim had studied in the evening newspaper on the day of his return: older, thinner and paler than he remembered, but with the same expression of short-sighted directness in the eyes, a glance which many took for arrogance.

'I thought you might be out,' he said, smiling with one corner of his mouth. The voice was the same; very deep but with the precise articulation of his generation. 'May I come in or is it inconvenient?'

Jim stepped back and opened the door, bowing his head slightly. He did not know what to say and instinctively fell back on old formalities.

'Come in, my Lord,' he said stiffly. 'I'm sorry to have kept you waiting but I was working.'

The bishop entered with slower, shorter steps than Jim remembered, leaning somewhat heavily on his umbrella. But he was still upright, and as he took off his hat the leonine mane of white hair was revealed; thick and strong as ever, springing up from the high forehead. He looked around the hall holding his hat against his chest.

'I'm upstairs, my Lord. There's no place here to hang your coat.' Jim plucked at the neck of his pullover, inside which he was wearing a bright red shirt. Dr Curley looked at him with a sudden twinkle in his eyes.

'I've taken off *my* red,' he said, opening his coat and unwinding his scarf. A plain black stock had taken the place of the episcopal scarlet under his Roman collar, and the small white hand which exposed it was ringless. He had removed one glove, and Jim wondered if this was from habit – how often had the missing ring been kissed during the past twenty-five years? On a sudden impulse he held out his hand and the bishop grasped it firmly and warmly. Jim turned hastily away and led his visitor upstairs. He was ashamed to find tears smarting his eyes but he had time to recover himself by the time they reached his flat.

'I suppose you're wondering why I came?' After taking off his coat the bishop rubbed his hands together and looked at the fire.

'I'm wondering that you came at all.' Jim's voice was hard, a reaction against the wave of emotion that had over-taken him in the hall. 'How did you find out where I was?'

'From Grace Condon.' The bishop used the Irish form of addressing a woman known to him from childhood by her maiden name.

'I'm surprised that she didn't tell me.'

'So that you could refuse?' The old man had lost none of his skill in debate. Jim was on the spot. Why had he admitted him, just now?

'Has Grace been talking to you about me?' Jim pushed one of the armchairs nearer the fire. Dr Curley had always loved a good fire. At conferences in the old days, fresh air fiends used to stagger out of the room panting.

'Yes, frequently. We've kept in touch. I used to drop in to

see her when I came up to Maynooth or Dublin. We often talked about you.' The bishop settled himself in the chair, resting his arms at full length and allowing his hands to hang over the edge: an episcopal gesture. Jim had a sudden vision of a book-lined study, a gothic window with the cathedral spire soaring over the trees outside, a high carved chair, and his visitor in red skull cap and sash, with the great pectoral cross of his office, sitting in just such an attitude with the big desk between them. Their last meeting. He had not expected to see the old man again.

'It's not like Grace to talk about her friends behind their backs.' Jim's voice was still sharp. He was well aware of how smoothly the bishop had bridged the years while he himself remained very much on the defensive.

'But very like her to talk well of them.' The bishop smiled, and bit his lip, the only clue he gave to a fundamental shyness.

'If it's necessary to talk about them at all in certain circumstances.' Not that he thought that Grace would ever criticise him to anyone. Nevertheless the idea of these two discussing him was not pleasant. 'You were keeping tabs on me.' He knew it sounded lame.

'If you like to put it like that. It seemed very natural to me, and to Grace too.'

'No doubt.' Jim's voice was dry.

'I wanted to call three years ago when the book on the Council came out, but she advised against it.'

'Have you no mind of your own?'

The bishop chuckled and shook his head, holding out a hand to the fire, the hard blue veins standing out like tiny inflated tubes under the wrinkled skin.

'That's the first time I've ever been accused of that, although I've often thought it myself.'

'And now for some reason she thinks you ought to.'

'Do you?' The old man looked up at Jim, who remained standing and his glance conveyed many things that remained unspoken between them. 'I called on her on my way here and told her I was coming. She didn't object. After all I'm no longer your bishop. I have thought of

97

you a great deal during the years, and prayed for you, for whatever that's worth. I acted according to my lights at the time and so did you. It is possible that we were both wrong. Besides I wanted to see you again before I go away.'

'Go away?' Jim was startled, and sat down without meaning to. 'Where?'

'We'll talk about that later.' He looked about the room, narrowed his eyes to peer at the bookcase and desk, on which the typewriter stood with its half-written sheet of paper propped against the extension arm. 'You're writing a new book.'

'You are well informed,' said Jim drily. 'I suppose Grace told you about that too.'

'As a matter of fact she didn't, but I can use my eyes. As I get older I can see better in the distance, which sometimes happens to short-sighted people. But I think I still screw my eyes up out of habit.' He gave Jim a wry look, not unmixed with regret. 'Habit is a hard thing to break.'

Before the younger man could consider the implications of this remark, which he felt was directed at him in some way, the door opened and Eddie burst in.

'Jim, I must talk to you, it's about Dolly ...' he broke off when he saw the old man in the armchair whom he did not immediately recognize. 'Oh, I'm terribly sorry. I didn't realize you had a visitor.' He backed out hastily and closed the door.

'He lives in the ground floor flat.' Jim, who was half way out of his chair, sat down again. 'I suppose Grace told you about him.' He was about to add 'too', but didn't.

'If it's young Doyle, yes. I thought his face was familiar. I knew his father well. Miss Keeley lives here too, doesn't she?'

'Yes.' Jim wondered how much the old man knew or guessed, but he was pretty sure that the relationship between Eddie and Maurice was one Grace would never discuss with anybody.

'I heard her singing once in Rome when I was in the Irish College. Not at the opera, of course, that was considered very sinful in those days. She came to dinner at

98

the Irish Embassy. Cardinal Gasparri was there, as I recall, it was just after the Lateran Treaty. She sang some Irish songs, Moore's melodies, you know. I'm afraid some of us wept. Those were the songs we used to sing at home when I was a boy.' He clasped his hands and stared into the fire as if he too were recalling sadly the light of other days.

Jim stood up and turned away, thinking what a bunch of sentimental bastards they all were. This was no time for emotions which, he suspected, he could no longer control. It was too ludicrous to think that anything could be resolved by getting tearful over a Victorian ballad, however well sung.

'We weren't afraid of sentiment in my day,' said the bishop suddenly.

'I don't suppose you've come for a drinking session,' Jim said briskly, 'but you'll have a little something, as they say?'

'I'm strictly forbidden it now.' The bishop tapped his chest. 'The old ticker. But if you give me a few drops of whiskey and put in plenty of water, I don't think that'll kill me. I don't want to die just now.'

Jim fixed the drink and poured a stiff brandy for himself. The bishop raised his glass and Jim responded before he sat down. He warmed his glass and waited. One struggle was over, he well knew. Another was about to begin.

III

He had not long to wait. Michael Curley was never a man to beat about the bush.

'You've heard of Tom Geraghty's death, I suppose.'

'Yes. He wrote to me shortly before.'

'I know. He told me the last time I was with him. It troubled him greatly. He blamed himself very much.'

'He needn't have. I'd forgotten about the whole thing.'

'No, you haven't. You wouldn't be human if you had. And if we forget everything, we wouldn't be able to forgive. Besides you wrote back to him. It was a very generous thing to do. No man who allowed his bitterness to get the better of him could ever have written a letter like that. And you have no idea how much it meant to Tom. He had a terrible death, you know. Cancer of the spine. But he was reconciled in the end. And for that, Jim, whether you like it or not, you're responsible.'

Jim clutched his brandy glass tightly and stared over the bishop's shoulder.

'He was only an agent. If it hadn't happened that way it would have come about in another, I wouldn't have stayed anyway.' He looked the other straight in the eye. 'I don't think you treated him very well afterwards. It's a bit of a shock to find yourself curate of the poorest and loneliest half-parish in the diocese, after being in the palace. We all thought he might wear your ring one day.'

'I'm Irish, Jim. I don't like informers any more than you do. But I regretted that also. I never seemed to do anything right. He lost his faith, you know. You didn't hear that? I didn't discover it either until near the end, in the hospital. But he continued on – mechanically. Perhaps it's another way of getting there, and besides he hadn't the same kind of temperament as you have. Everything came too easily to him in the beginning. And when it was tested it went just as easily. In the end it was you who fixed him up, not me. So you were an agent too.'

'You were always a dab hand at turning a man's words

100

back at him, my Lord. I should have remembered that.' He sipped his drink and felt his tongue burning.

'How can we tell? Maybe Tom would have been reconciled anyway. It might have been a greater thing, alone. But that's the way it turned out. And as for turning your words back on you, you didn't give me much chance at any time. I think the way poor Tom acted hit you harder than you have ever admitted, even to yourself.'

Jim looked up sharply, sensing danger. The preliminaries were over. But the bishop was sipping his weak whiskey and water. Much as he would like to have remained silent Jim could not prevent himself from asking the question he felt the other was waiting for.

'Do you mean that you would have been able to persuade me to change my views and disown the book, if you had found out about it in some other way?'

Dr Curley smiled and wiped the corner of his mouth with his thumb.

'I would have tried. After all we only discussed it twice. I thought it was wrong, and I still do. I had to do my duty. I thought that by putting you through the ropes, it would give you time to think. Of course I knew old Smiley would reject it. He took his role of censor very seriously, especially since it was honorary – if that's the word to describe it. No book had been written by a priest in our diocese for forty years, and even then that was a local history of holy wells. If you had written a pamphlet for the Catholic Truth Society he'd have condemned it, if you tried to get it published without my imprimatur. So I sent it to Lennon of Killoughlan (mentioning the name of a diocesan censor well known for his liberal views) and even he balked at it. There didn't seem to be anything for it except send it to Rome.'

'Lennon advised that also?'

'Yes. But he suggested that I should have a talk with you beforehand and tell you. I did and, as you know, asked you to carry on until we saw what would happen. I knew what the Holy Office would say, or the Congregation for the Doctrine of the Faith as they call it now. But I thought that by talking to you, and thrashing it out, you might change your mind, or at least modify your views. But you didn't give me time. You just disappeared.'

'What would have been the point of staying? I knew it would be condemned and I wasn't prepared to go through all that process in Rome. And besides, no one is ever convinced by argument, are they?'

'Precisely. I knew what would happen, and that you would be interrogated. So I didn't send it to Rome, Father. So far as Rome is concerned, it's just a book by someone called Mark Denson, who might be a layman. I don't suppose they've ever heard of it and if they have, they've certainly forgotten it by now.'

'You didn't send it to Rome.' Jim pronounced every word slowly and distinctly as if he were trying to master a very simple lesson by repeating it like a child.

'No, I intended to talk it over with you. I found it very interesting. At least you were trying to discover something. But I never had the opportunity of finding out what it was, until now. Which is why I'm here.'

Jim got up and walked across the room to the windows, the bookcase, the desk. He was hardly aware of them, scarcely conscious of the glass he held in his hand. He did not even smell the brandy. The world had shrunk to an exchange of words between two men in a room that might just as well have been bare, in a house whose other inhabitants he had forgotten, in a city which could be any place in the world.

'It's pretty generally known now who I am, although I've gone on using the same nom-de-plume. Rome may be a bit slow on the uptake, but it's not as remote as all that. I gave my reasons for leaving in black and white.' He lifted his drink and absent-mindedly began to swallow it like beer.

'Things have changed. They have more on their minds now than your particular theory of original sin. And your other books have been read by Lennon, and by me. He would have no hesitation in passing them in the present climate – I mean the last two – and I would give them an imprimatur, except that I'm not in that particular line of

102

business any more. But that is not the point now, is it?'

'No.' Jim came out of his haze, felt the swallowed brandy warming his stomach, and walked back to his chair to sit down. 'No, it is not.'

'You were never silenced in the ordinary way, certainly not by me, and no one else had the authority. Not even Rome.'

A few minutes before the bishop had called him 'Father'. He realized now that it was the shock of hearing that again after so many years, and the discovery that no official action had been taken over the book that produced the sensation of disassociation. Beyond the dogmas, the hierarchical institution, all the accumulated trappings of an ancient tradition there was something else; deep, mysterious, inevitable, which was gradually filling his consciousness as the brandy warmed his bones. Something stark, yet tender, pertinacious and all-pervading.

'No,' he said doggedly, 'it was swept under the carpet.'

'There is something to be said for that in many ways, human nature being what it is. We are, if you remember your own theory, animals with souls. Why set dog against dog? We all have enough trouble in keeping the beast under the skin as it is.'

Jim laughed, quietly but with a sense of appreciation. His own words neatly turned back on him again.

'Besides, as I said before, you didn't wait, even for a fight. Unless I'm mistaken you've asked yourself a lot of questions in the last ten years. What answers have you come up with?'

'What answers have you?'

'I gave up asking questions a long time ago.'

'That's no answer.'

'No. But then I very much doubt if life is merely a series of questions and answers.'

'How about the word "why"? Haven't you ever asked yourself that?'

'Frequently. But I never really succeeded in answering it. Oh, there are all kinds of theological arguments. One could go on hair-splitting like that for a lifetime. In the end you accept a mystery, or you don't. So we've both come to the same conclusion, by different routes.'

'What makes you think that?' Jim resisted the assumption with a stare.

'It was in your first book. And it certainly is in your last two. I was taught the traditional doctrine of the Fall. You called it animal ignorance. Whatever it is, or was, I don't think you'd deny that there's an accumulation of evil in the world, and there's only one answer to that – charity. As well as tolerance, self-denial and restraint, which you also mentioned.'

'Have you become a heretic in your old age, my Lord?'

'Curiously enough I thought you'd come out with that sooner or later. You're just the man to do it. Like those priests who want to get married but would be horrified if the Pope got there before them.'

'It's a good thing we didn't have this talk ten years ago.' Jim swallowed the rest of his brandy. 'I might have stayed on.'

The bishop chuckled and shook his head.

'You might. And you might not. I think it was better the way it was. We belong to different generations. I accepted authority without question, and used it the same way. Which is why I think less about it now, and you think more. You've discovered what kind the world is when you face it alone. Misery, despair, doubt, self-hatred, and the emptiness of pride. You begin to think some kind of order is necessary, although it may not be the sort I represented in my hey-day.'

Jim thought of the paragraph just completed before he went down to admit his visitor. In the old days he had always liked the bishop, and felt that the old boy had taken a paternal interest in him. Even when the storm broke he was given a sympathetic hearing. No bitter words had ever been exchanged between them, and he knew how Geraghty's treachery had been rewarded. But in former days, age, authority, canon law and the custom of the country inhibited any real communication between them.

'Is that why you retired?' he said, not without a touch of malice.

'Partly. I was too old to break down the barriers. I couldn't do it with you, although I'd have tried if you'd let me. But the system was against us. So it was time to get out. Besides there's something else I want to do.'

Jim's face stiffened, and the bishop held up his hand.

'No, it's not to "fix you up", as they say. That's something you'll have to do for yourself. You know what you are, and what you will be until the day you die. The same applies to me. So I thought I'd try and make myself useful. I think I've got a few years yet, with the help of God. So I'm going to South America.'

'As a priest?' said Jim stupidly, startled by this piece of unexpected information.

'Well, what else? You don't expect me to go as a white slave trader, do you? There's a shortage of them out there – priests, I mean. At least I can hear confessions and say Mass.'

'When are you going?' Jim put down his glass very slowly.

'I'd like to see the new fellow installed. You know him. He was a class-mate of yours at Maynooth.'

'Jack Wilson? He and Tom and I used to pal around together.'

'He's quite an admirer of yours, you know. I wouldn't be at all surprised if he turned up on your doorstep someday too.'

'So you'll be going fairly soon?'

'Well, there are a number of things I've got to fix up. My sister is almost crippled now, so I'm getting her into a Nazareth Home. And there are all sorts of other things. Then there's the language. Portuguese. I've been studying it for the past year on records but I'm going to a mission school outside Dublin for a while, for conversation and that. I'm not finding it too easy but it's coming along. All in all I'd say it'll be four to six months before I get going.'

Jim stared at his empty glass. For some inexplicable reason a scene he had witnessed as a boy came back into his mind. He had thought of it often before, always in moments of blank despair. A little boy standing at the door of a shop on a windy day with a wad of brown tissue paper in his hand, tearing off strips and throwing them into the air, to be whirled wildly down the street. The son of the man whose shop they dealt in. How he had envied him his possession of such riches.

'You have a nice place here,' said the bishop, breaking into his thoughts.

'Where exactly are you going?'

'Sao Paulo. A slum parish, I believe. They reckon that one look at me will scare the gizzards out of any tough elements there. The cops are not so keen on us there just now. One look at me and they'll think it's Mayor Daley.'

'So you'll be in Dublin off and on during the next few months?'

'Yes. Is that an invitation to call again, or would you rather wait for Jack Wilson?'

'Why should I do that? It started with you, and it might as well finish there.'

The bishop heaved himself to his feet. There was a twinkle in his eye.

'In that case, will you introduce me to Miss Keeley? I'd like to meet her again. I wonder if she remembers that dinner party?'

'Her memory,' said Jim, going to fetch the bishop's coat, 'is as good as mine.'

IV

'You poor thing.' The La pulled a Moroccan embroidered hassock in front of Dolly's chair. 'Take your shoes off and put your feet up here.'

'I'm that weak, I don't know what way I am.' Dolly's voice was shaking. She was ashen pale, and trembling. In the ordinary course Maria would not have offered her a drink again, but she had no heart to refuse her now. Something would have to be done about the real problem later.

'Does your husband know?' she said as she went to the big black Florentine chest where she kept her treasured ornaments and the bottles of wines and liqueurs which were given her as presents from time to time. She knew that the question was ambiguous and rather hoped that Dolly would come clean.

'How could he? He's up on Border duty. Besides he wasn't with me when I fell off the bus.' She fixed her eyes on the gorgeous but tattered kimono which hung on the wall over the chest. Maria's costume for 'Butterfly', crucified by time. Her little living room was covered with them. Mimi's simple dress on one side of the window, Desdemona's rich robe for the first act of 'Otello' on the other, while on the end wall facing the fireplace was spread out the magnificent blue cloak she wore in 'Manon Lescaut'.

The La sighed as she poured out a glass of brandy. Even if her visitor had blurted out a confession, Maria Keeley was ill equipped to deal with it. Alcoholism was almost unknown in Italy and certainly in women. She wished Maurice was at home – he knew all about it – but would he want to have anything to do with Dolly? It was doubtful.

'Oh, thank you, Miss Keeley. This will help me to pull myself together. Haven't you the lovely things,' she went on to distract attention as she gulped down her drink. Dolly's eye had caught the gleam of Eddie's gold snuff-box on the carved chest.

The ploy worked admirably, although it did not get Dolly another drink. Having had the box for a week The La was now quite convinced that it was hers. Dolly's instinct for camouflage, so often developed to an uncanny pitch by alcoholics, had not failed her. The La took the trophy up and gazed at it lovingly.

'It was given me by Rico Orsini,' she explained in her most plaintive nostalgic voice. 'Prince Orsini, you know. They are one of the oldest families in Italy. Look here, on the lid, is a miniature of one of his ancestors.'

Dolly took it wonderingly and looked at the portrait of the handsome young man. It was in fact the likeness of the son of a rich Parisian merchant in the reign of Louis Philippe. Eddie's father, remembering the gold sovereigns of his youth driven out of circulation by the First World War, had bought the snuff-box as an investment in Paris in 1920.

They admired it back and forth for some time while The La explained how the Prince had wanted to marry her, in spite of having a wife already.

'He wanted me to elope with him to America, get a divorce there, and settle in the wild west. He was furbo. Such a thing was impossible.'

She was shaken out of her reconstruction of the past by the sight of Dolly's darned skirt, her wet hair and sodden shoes and something lost and desperate in her eyes. Jim was upstairs. She would go to him, have a little talk and bring him down to meet his poverina. Perhaps he might be able to suggest something. As an Irish priest, however unorthodox, he would surely know all about alcoholics.

'Ah, yes,' she said, taking the box and putting it back on the chest again, 'It's worth a fortune. Even I do not want a burial as big as this will buy when my time comes. But now rest your ankles, cara, I have to go upstairs for a few minutes. When I come back we will have a little talk.'

Dolly watched the door close with glistening eyes. She wanted to cry but she craved a drink even more. She stood up and darted to the chest to pour herself another glass of brandy, caught her breath to save herself from a fit of choking, and tossed it back. Would she have time for another? She thought of the unbearable evening at home, for she had run out of everything, and there was no prospect of further credit from any of the publicans she knew. Then her eyes alighted on the snuff-box. She snatched it up, ran back to the chair, slipped her foot into her shoe, thrust the object into her bag and made for the door. She could think of nothing now except the insatiable craving that consumed her. There was a money lender in York Street who would give her something for it: twenty, thirty pounds perhaps. She might even get more, enough to keep her going for the next few days and pay off the most pressing of the bills in her bag. She hurried out, crept up the stairs, and waited with thumping heart for a sound from above. Even if Miss Keeley did come down, she was not likely to inspect her bag, and she could make an excuse that she had to hurry home to get the children's tea.

She was out the front door and turning into Lower Leeson Street before The La descended, leading a reluctant Jim in her wake; and already turning into the money lender's in York Street before Maria discovered that her precious gold snuff-box was missing. Shrieking, she called Jim down again, and the pair of them were standing in the hall, The La bewailing her loss in operatic tones, when Eddie came in.

'My snuff-box, my snuff-box,' she cried when she saw him. 'It's been taken, whipped from under my nose by that Dolly Hughes. Your friend. A fortune's worth, given to me by Rico Orsini, with a family portrait on the lid. You must ring her husband at once and get it back.'

'*Your* snuff-box,' said Eddie weakly. 'Dolly?' He looked at Jim, who shook his head.

'Well, do something,' screamed The La. 'Don't stand there gaping. At once, d'you hear me? Right under my very nose, the drunken, stealing little slut. If you don't I'll report it to the Guards myself. This moment. Santo Dio! Sangue di Dio! What a crew.'

V

'How much is it worth?' said Jim.

'I don't know.' Eddie looked at Maurice who was huddled in the armchair next to the table on which the snuff-box had been placed before The La filched it. He was looking weaker and more exhausted than usual, but was obviously trying to take an interest in the proceedings. He looked at Eddie and moistened his dry bloodless lips.

'Five or six hundred, I'd say, if one was to buy it from a dealer. Maybe more. But she's probably hocked it for a tenner, or sold it outright for even less. A woman in that state will do anything.'

'Perhaps you'd better ring again,' said Jim. 'She might have bought a couple of bottles and gone home.'

Eddie dialed the number. He had already rung up twice since they heard the news: once at half-six, and again at nine. A few minutes before ten The La departed, threatening dire consequences if her property was not recovered.

May answered again. Her voice was timid and frightened as it had been when she answered before. Eddie now knew the reason why the children had behaved so curiously the last time he had visited the Hugheses. They realized something was wrong with their mother, although he doubted if even May understood exactly what it was.

'Is your Mammy home yet May? he asked gently. 'This is Eddie.'

'No.' The girl's voice trembled and she burst into tears.

'Now, now, don't worry May.' Eddie's high, tense voice was a far from soothing one. 'She's only at the station waiting for your Daddy. She got word he might be home tonight.'

'She is not,' stammered May through her tears. 'She's up in McCarvill's pub and she won't be home till half-eleven. And me Daddy won't be home till tomorrow.' She rang off, leaving Eddie with a slight feeling of relief. This was a conversation he would not have been able to sustain a moment longer.

110

'I suppose the child knows,' said Jim quietly. 'They nearly always do. We'll just have to wait until Greg gets home. Ring up the Guards' barracks first thing in the morning. Otherwise he might get into serious trouble. It all depends what she's done with the thing.' He stood up and looked at Maurice. 'She'll get home somehow. They usually do.'

'And never have an accident. And in the morning she'll have a story ready and a half bottle of gin to get her going. I wouldn't be at all surprised if she's been fooling the husband for years. But you're probably right about the kids. I've heard that you can't pull it off with them. Fortunately I never had to.'

'I wish to God I'd never seen the bloody thing,' burst out Eddie when Jim had gone. He sat down and held his head in his hands.

'No, you don't.' Maurice looked about the room searchingly, as if he wanted to impress every detail of it in his mind. Eddie had noticed him doing it frequently recently; and it frightened him. 'It belonged to your mother. You wouldn't sell it for a thousand.'

'If I'd only got it back from The La, but I was . . .' he broke off and covered his eyes by clasping his hand against his forehead. He had made several half-hearted attempts to get into Maria's flat during the past week, but he had been too preoccupied worrying about Maurice to exercise his usual ingenuity. He had recovered his Sevres vase by the simple expedient of telling her that a reporter from the *London Times* was in the hall looking for her. When she discovered the trick there had been a terrible row and she had not spoken to him for a week. He made it up by a gift of Floris bath essence and a more than usually barbaric necklace of costume jewellery.

Maurice knew exactly what Eddie meant. That morning he had fainted in the shop and the previous afternoon Dr Isaacson had advised him to go into hospital and offered to get him a bed.

'So much for your happy family,' he said, pulling out his tie and lowering his nose to sniff his chest. It seemed to him that lately his flesh gave off a curiously sweet, almost sugary odour which disgusted him more than the alcoholic vomit in which he had sprawled more than once in his life.

Eddie looked up in surprise. Quite often recently Maurice had drawn him out on the subject of the Hugheses and the Fitzgeralds. It almost seemed as if he were trying to enter into this aspect of Eddie's life, to draw from him the secret of how he admired and adapted himself so easily and enthusiastically to lives so different from his own. Although Eddie was only too happy to talk, he did so with a good deal of uneasiness. They had always respected one another's prejudices. Now it seemed that the dying man was reaching out, searching for that corner of Eddie's heart which had always been closed to him, because he demanded it that way, and open to others.

'They *were* happy,' he protested. 'I'm sure of that. I don't know what has come over Dolly. But I know that Greg will stand by her, no matter what happens.'

'They were happy because you wanted them to be.' Maurice settled his tie inside his waistcoat and lay back in his chair. 'And of course they played up. Naturally Greg will stand by her. Have you ever heard of a divorced Guard in this country? The most he'll do is put her in St John of God's, and everyone will look the other way. That's the only method by which they can get through life – pretending. How do you know what she really thinks of him, or he of her?'

'I never thought happiness consisted of a series of picnics in the sun with everybody forgetting their troubles while the rest of the world went puck.'

'That's where you're wrong. The only way you can exist at all is to let the rest of the world go puck. We've had our picnics.'

'What about The La, and Jim, and Grace and Desmond? Our world isn't large, but they belong to it.'

'Have you ever tried telling them about us in plain language? I bet you haven't. They all know, but do they approve? They all pretend not to notice. Pretence, all pretence.'

112

'And yet you trusted *me*,' said Eddie quietly, thinking that although he had not told Grace 'in plain language', he had nevertheless told her.

Unexpectedly Maurice smiled, the grin of self-depreciation that is sometimes seen on the face of a man who has won a bet.

'Perhaps one person is enough,' said Eddie tentatively, hoping that Maurice would admit some sort of acceptance of the larger vision. 'I mean to make one trust others too.'

'If you're lucky enough to meet one.' Again the slightly puzzled grin. 'I took a gamble, and it paid off. I had nothing to lose. It proves nothing.'

'What can anyone prove?' began Eddie and broke off. Once again they were faced with a mystery, which he accepted with a kind of grateful wonder, but which Maurice maintained stubbornly was the result of blind chance. To him they were a couple of lucky gamblers, who having won the first throw had left the tables early and invested their winnings. In a way this was true. But it did not explain the long gradual process of mutual trust and inter-dependence which they had experienced.

Even Eddie, who was easily affected by sentiment and much given to piety about the past, never attempted to soften the memory of their first months together. It had been a growth accompanied by many set-backs. From the beginning both sensed something in the other which he himself lacked and wanted to possess. For Eddie it was the discovery of a stoical vein of endurance which he attributed to Maurice's intense masculinity, while he himself was capable of a natural spontaneity and sympathy which Maurice lacked. But it was his truthfulness and honesty, qualities which Maurice admired above all others and had ceased to believe possible at the time of their meeting, that had gradually broken down the barriers between them, allowing other and more important ones to take their place. Suspicion gave way to admiration, and admiration to trust.

They saved themselves from early disaster by a recognition of certain limits which both respected. If they had met ten years earlier they might easily have destroyed each other. But they were neither innocent nor inexperienced and both had been scarred by the cold-hearted promiscuity of the half-world they were forced to inhabit because of their emotional needs.

On both sides there was violent physical attraction which Eddie, possessing a far more sensual and uninhibited nature, accepted at once. The mental barriers down, many mutual interests in music and literature discovered, they were faced with the ultimate expression of passion, human and demanding, in spite of its unorthodox form. If they had understood each other less, they would not have been so afraid of it. But Maurice had a deep-rooted sense of puritanical reserve, and Eddie a delicate and sensitive awareness of the terrible vulnerability of their involvement. So precious was their friendship, with its underlying tensions, that he had almost accepted the fact that it must always remain platonic.

Eddie knew Maurice for nearly a year before the top flat became vacant and he prevailed upon him to move into it, after recommending him in sober and diplomatic terms to Desmond and Grace. Both men knew what this move implied. Neither could think how it would work out. But they could no longer imagine a life in which they were separated.

Unable to suppress a nature both sensual and affectionate, Eddie made the first move. And had been struck down by the brutal violence possible only to those who see in another, adored and idolised, the same human frailty which they despise in themselves. Yet that savage blow had resolved their shy and cautious dilemma.

Eddie's remorse was so quiet and self-effacing, his shame at his own maladroit expression of something so deeply felt, that Maurice had been touched. Some unscarred corner of his heart responded to his friend's misery and in his awkward fumbling efforts to make amends, the dam had broken and they were both swept away by a tide that was all the more irresistible for being held back for so long. It seemed to them at the time that they were comforting each other; a recompense which they owed to one another as outcasts and allies in a hostile world.

Maurice in particular was surprised by the depths of his own feeling. Nothing in his previous experience had prepared him for the wonder he discovered in this total commitment. To him it appeared an act of such protective tenderness and unspoken longing that all his doubts, agonies and furtive desires were stilled by the justice of it. It seemed like some act of retribution meted out by a capricious fate, suddenly and inexplicably contrite. Justice indeed. And for once unutterably sweet. He did not know that he was tasting – late, and with more intensity than is possible for those to whom such mysteries are revealed early and easily – all the rapture, gratitude and unselfishness that lovers have experienced since the world began. For him it was too precious, too private even to talk about. Only once in all the years that followed, years in which they grew to know and respect the rules of love, had Maurice mentioned it.

'We're going to pay for this some day,' he said gloomily. 'Life doesn't hand out bonuses like this for nothing. Not to people like us anyway.'

'Don't be silly,' replied Eddie, who had never felt the slightest guilt in the realization of his instincts and adapted himself to certain reticences quite willingly, but out of loyalty to his friend. 'Love is indivisible.'

Maurice frowned at this and said nothing further. Now that remark came back into Eddie's mind as they sat alone after his call about Dolly. He did not believe that they were paying for anything. What had happened to Maurice could have happened to anyone. They had kept their unspoken pledge. It only remained for him to keep his to the bitter end. After that he did not want to think.

'I think I'll go to bed.' Maurice got up slowly. As they went upstairs Eddie slipped his arm through his friend's and pressed it gently. The shrunken flesh responded and Eddie's eyes blurred with tears as he felt the appalling thinness of the arm. They were back where they had begun; in a communion beyond the body.

115

'Stay with me tonight, Eddie. Please. I'm horrible now, but ...'

Eddie pressed his arm again, and snatched at justice for the last time.

VI

The next day was the last that Maurice worked. After lunch he collapsed in the shop and was brought home in a taxi: conscious and able to get to his room, slowly and unaided, but too weak to undress. He lay on the bed and looked at Jim who had come up when he heard the footsteps on the stairs.

'I think you ought to get into bed properly, Maurice. I'll give you a hand.'

'No, I'll stay like this for a while. Just get me a glass of water and that bottle of blue pills on the dressing-table.'

After he had swallowed his pills and handed back the glass Maurice looked at Jim with his fixed glassy stare.

'Shall I call Isaacson?'

'No. Not yet. He won't be free until five anyway, and I know what he's going to say when he comes. What I'd like to hear is what you have to say.'

Jim sat down and looked at the blue, careless February sky through the window. It was a long time since he had been alone with Maurice. The two men were wary of each other; both proud, puritanical, with a dogged determination to preserve their own integrity at any cost.

'I haven't got any answers, Maurice, if that's what you're looking for.'

'Except the old ones.'

'You know them.'

'As well as you do.' In spite of his weakened condition Maurice's voice was still strong. Jim had enough experience of sick beds to know that this was often the last to go. The bare room, so like his own in many ways, made him feel more uncomfortable still by its sweetish smell of sickness. It brought him back to other rooms where he had given conventional answers. 'Pray for me, Father, I can't remember anymore.' 'Don't worry, God is merciful. So long as you trust him.' It was amazing how often it worked; wonderful the solace of seeing the body accepting the dread mystery of dissolution in reconciliation. But there was nothing he

117

could do here. Those others had been fearful, but they had hoped.

He made a movement to get up intending to call The La. But some words that he had often repeated to himself in his early days, flashed suddenly through his mind. 'Stay with us, because it is towards evening, and the day is now far spent.' And the other words so often repeated on the far side of the tomb: 'Fear not.'

'Yes, stay a bit,' said Maurice. 'I'm not afraid. I only hope this thing doesn't go on too long. It's quite easy when you're very tired. And I've been tired of myself for a long time.'

'You shouldn't be.' Jim felt more composed. Perhaps this was the answer. Maurice had never accepted himself. And he was bringing his hatred of the God that made him to the edge of the grave. Jim felt powerless, but there was a ray of hope. He thought of Eddie. Love of any kind was better than no love at all. 'You have better friends than many people. Some have to make do with none at all.'

'Eddie? I thought we'd get round to him. Because he accepted me as I am, or was, you think I ought to be grateful.'

'Aren't you?' Jim could not conceal his surprise and Maurice smiled wanly.

'Oh, he accepted me, all right. Do you know that he stayed here with me last night?' Maurice wrinkled his nose and fumbled with his tie. 'I smell of death, but he stayed with me. You know about us, I suppose in that way?'

Jim nodded. It was too late to mend fences now.

'But you very charitably kept your mouth shut about it, you and The La, and Grace and Desmond. But when I'm gone?'

'I don't understand.' Jim was genuinely puzzled, but he did not know that the look he gave the waxen face turned towards him on the pillow contained a flash of hostility.

'Oh, we didn't commit your kind of sin last night. I've been past that for some time now. He accepted me as he always does. But do you think that I have done the same with him?'

Jim was still puzzled. He felt that the other was trying to tell him something he would never have expressed in any other condition.

'When I'm gone you all think he'll be left alone.'

'He will. Very much alone.'

'Do you think he'll forget me?'

'I think it's very unlikely.'

'I have never accepted him, you know. Not completely.' Maurice raised himself on one elbow and leaned forward, his sunken eyes bright with sickness. 'He's too soft-hearted, too trusting for your world. I've tried to make him see how false and cruel it really is. There is no other way of facing it.'

'I think there is.'

'I know you do. And you and all the rest of them will try to make him see it that way. But he promised to let me leave this world in my own way. That is something that none of you will ever succeed in making him forget. Because to do that he'd have to accept your belief.'

Jim sprang to his feet, upsetting his chair in his confusion. It scraped the boards with a sound like bone upon bone.

'You can't do that,' he said sharply. 'What you believe is your own business. But you have no right to impose it on another. You can hate the world as much as you like, there are times when we all do. Don't imagine we're going to force you to do anything you don't want to do. Your soul is your own business. But so is Eddie's.'

'There is no such thing. Had your Man any right to tell his followers to eat his flesh? There is only memory, and the bits and pieces of flesh and bone we drag about us for a few years here without knowing why. So long as Eddie lives he will have to remember me that way. It's the only way I'll accept him in the end, and he knows it.'

As Jim stared at the emaciated face pointed towards him, the bloodless mouth twisted with passionate defiance, he wondered for a moment if Maurice's wits were going astray. But what did he know of the secret life of these two men, or of the tie which bound them together? He had often

119

admired it. But never before had he realized the enormity of the rejection which on Maurice's part at least, made it possible. Such tortured involvement, which attempted the possession of the soul of another, was beyond his comprehension. And yet he was bound to believe in faith that all that was best in the dying man had been expressed in his devotion to Eddie: the only love of which he was capable. Was it possible that a man could ever destroy that? It was not for him to judge. Then he caught himself up, recollecting that the idea 'in faith' had passed through his mind. Could it be that this man, apparently so full of hatred of himself, had succeeded in breaking the last barrier which separated the ex-priest from all he had left behind? For now he knew that indeed he believed 'in faith', and that he would remember the circumstances of its final acceptance all his life. Eddie was not the only one who would not forget Maurice. The strange currents of life, so arbitrarily catalogued by those who dabble in the unconscious, were turning and twisting about him. His resistance to them in the past had almost drowned him. Now he suddenly relaxed, the tension within him eased, and he felt himself open, defenceless and strangely happy. He knew that he would go on asking questions – the mystery of this man's rejection among them – but he knew now that he would no longer expect any answers.

Maurice's face changed, he fell back gasping. Jim hurried to his side, felt his pulse, then ran downstairs for The La.

VII

When Greg turned up that evening at seven much had been arranged and accomplished. Jim phoned Isaacson, who hurried across the street between patients, gave Maurice an injection, and said he would call again on his way home. He met Eddie in the hall on his second visit, advised an immediate removal to the hospital, and both of them went up to the sick man. He had recovered consciousness after the doctor's first call, and was talking to The La, who remained with him after Jim undressed him, put on his pyjamas and got him into bed. Isaacson pronounced him out of danger for the moment, but told Eddie and Jim on his way out that the end could come at any time during the next month – or sooner.

Eddie would not hear of the hospital. Jim and the doctor exchanged glances and did not press the point when he insisted that a day-nurse should be installed, while he himself would have a bed set up in the front room and look after Maurice during the night. Isaacson promised to do his best to get a private nurse, but was not enthusiastic about the idea. However, he felt that it would not help matters to order a removal just then. He would get the woman, and wait and see how things worked out for a few days. The anemia was far advanced and the fever high. It was miraculous that Maurice had kept on his feet so long but the doctor felt that this would hasten the end. There was nothing for it but to administer as much amethopterin as the patient would take.

After he had gone, Eddie, white and shaken, but surprisingly calm set about making arrangements for the dismantling of his bed and its removal upstairs.

In her agitation The La completely forgot about the missing snuff-box, and so did Eddie. He was downstairs, pulling out drawers aimlessly in his bedroom when the door bell rang, and for a moment he thought of not answering it. But it might be Dr Isaacson again or the nurse.

121

'Oh,' he said when he opened the door to Greg, 'how did you hear?'

'You left a message for me. And I've been home.'

'Oh, yes of course, I forgot. Come in. It seemed terrible last night, but now ...' he sighed and shook his head.

'But it *is* terrible, Eddie. What am I going to do?'

Confused as he was, the bewilderment in Greg's voice and the frightened look in his yellow eyes brought Eddie back to the reality of another tragedy, no less real to Hughes than Maurice's state was to him. He sat down, motioned Greg to a chair and looked helplessly into the flickering fire.

'She's in an awful state,' Greg went on miserably. 'She told me everything. I don't know what to say. Is Miss Keeley going to make a charge?'

'Of course not,' said Eddie dully. 'The thing belongs to me. The La borrowed it, as usual. How is Dolly?'

'I had to get the doctor. He gave her something before I came away. But I pieced things together before. I've suspected it for some time, but I never realized it was so bad. She's been an alcoholic for about a year, and I – I don't understand it. The kids are frightened out of their lives, and she's run up bills all over the place.'

'I'm sorry Greg. I'm not quite taking it all in. You see, Maurice collapsed this afternoon. It's only a question of time.'

Greg could not have looked more miserable than he was. But in spite of himself he felt a sense of relief that Eddie's preoccupied manner was not entirely the result of Dolly's action.

'I'm sorry,' he said mechanically. 'It's an awful fucking world.' But the tone of his voice, although it reflected his own troubles, was stricken enough to arouse Eddie. In a way it took his mind off his own situation. He got up, poured himself a drink and handed a whiskey to Greg. In his heavy Crombie overcoat, under which he had pulled on a sports jacket over his uniform trousers and shirt, the big man looked tired, seedy and desperate.

'Did you find out what she did with it?' Eddie said

briskly enough, as he sat on the arm of the sofa and tried to interest himself in this now quite irrelevant business.

'She took it to a money-lender and sold it for twenty pounds. I know him and I can get it back from him. He's a bit of a receiver too, money-lending is only one of his rackets.'

'You'll have to pay him. Have you the money?'

'I have twenty pounds.' Greg did not mention that he had borrowed ten of it from a colleague until next pay day.

'But supposing he makes trouble? It might be better to leave it to him, especially if he denies it. I'm not going to say anything and The La will have forgotten it by now.'

'He won't make trouble,' said Greg grimly. 'I have enough on this fellow to land him in the Joy for the next twelve months.'

'But supposing Dolly signed anything? You can't bring any pressure on him if your own wife is involved.'

'Oh, can't I? If she signed anything – and she can't remember whether she did or not – he'll hand it over to me, or else – it's good enough for him to get his fucking twenty quid back. He knows the ropes.'

'I don't know how it happened,' went on Greg, wiping his mouth with the back of his hand. 'It's not my fault that I'm away from home so often. And the way she deceived me right under my nose. I thought it was nerves. But why should this happen to us? Why?'

'Why should anything happen to anybody, Greg?' said Eddie sadly. He felt no consolation that this man, who seemed to him so blessed by nature, was now as bewildered as himself. 'But you'll have to stand by her now. She needs help. There may be no reason for it at all. Perhaps she just took a drink or two to keep up and then got into the habit of it. Some people haven't the temperament for it.' He thought of Maurice. Odd that Dolly and he should be involved in the same problem. But Maurice had worked his way out without any help from anyone. No wonder he distrusted the rest of the world.

'I don't even know how she got on to this bloody money-lender,' went on Greg, following his own train of thought. 'I

123

never mentioned his name at home. She must have heard about him in one of the pubs.'

'Where did she get the money for all this?' said Eddie absently.

'Isn't that what I was telling you? She hasn't paid the grocer for the last six months, and she has a stack of bills from all the publicans round Dalkey in her bag. Even if this hadn't happened I'd hear about it soon. As it is I don't know how she did it, except that she was trading on my name. And we always paid our way until now.' He swallowed the last of his drink and coughed into his fist. He had caught a cold on the Border.

'Have you an idea of how much it is?'

'Only roughly. The sight of the bills frightened the life out of me. I'd say it's more than eight hundred.' Greg's voice sank to an awed whisper. He had never had that much money in one piece in his life.

'Good God! What are you going to do?'

'I don't know. I've borrowed on my insurance policy already. That was after the baby was born. There was always something and I just couldn't keep up with it. But I thought I had cleared up everything then.'

Eddie thought of his snuff-box. It seemed fated. He would find out what it really was worth as soon as he could. He knew an art-dealer with whom he once had an affair. A bitch, but honest.

'Well, go and get that blasted box back if you can. We'll talk about Dolly later.'

'I'll leave it in on my way home.' Greg rose heavily to his feet and picked up his hat.

'Ring my bell, and if you get no reply ring Jim's or Maurice's. On no account must The La get her hands on it.' Suddenly he giggled, and Greg stared at him incredulously. He did not realize that people often laugh at the incongruous in the very face of death. There is a certain smile more ominous than tears and The La had an Italian proverb: when the omens are good, take care, when they are bad, rejoice.

'I'll see to that.' Greg was shocked as he prepared to go

124

about his distasteful business. But after all, how could a fellow like Eddie, who had never wanted for anything in his life, be expected to understand real trouble?

VIII

'What is Dublin?' said Grace.

'A state of mind,' replied Jim in the same preoccupied tone. They were standing at one of the windows of his flat, looking down on the square. It was a clear frosty day. The houses, varying in colour from dark brown to light red were slashed with rays of slanting sunshine. The lawn of the park, where the tennis courts had once been, was acid green. The tops of some of the parked cars reflected dazzling discs of light which made both of them screw up their eyes from time to time. Beyond, the roofs of the city they lived in, but did not greatly love, spread out invisible to them, but forming different impressions in their minds. Jim thought of the pea-soup Liffey, the spires and domes rippling from the clouds which reflected the bay, while the bay itself crinkled like a mackerel sky. And the mountains too lazy to soar. Grace idly conjured up Dublin smells; a whiff of tidal river, tar from boats, and as always coffee at Islandbridge.

'Did you ever hear of Wadelai?' said Jim.

'No, where is it?'

'I heard it last year. It's some place beyond Drumcondra. I've always meant to go and see if it's true, although it's on the map.'

'Sounds like a south sea island.'

Decidedly they were not thinking of Dublin, and like true country-people were well aware that both knew of the game.

It was an interlude and they were both tired. Since Maurice's collapse a week ago, Grace came in almost every day, and Jim was up and down to the sick room constantly. The nurse was installed; stone deaf but efficient. Isaacson wrote out her instructions and she fulfilled them meticulously. Although she looked as frail as paper she was able to turn Maurice in the bed unaided, shave him and display great agility in running up and down stairs. Surprisingly he seemed to enjoy it and pronounced her the best barber he had ever had. She drifted in and out of the house like smoke. Grace thought she looked like a spectre of death but did not express it. She was glad they succeeded in getting someone for Eddie's sake.

'He looks very weak today,' she said, turning back into the room. The typewriter was missing from the desk. People were dropping in and out so often now that Jim was working very early in the morning down in Eddie's flat, for fear that his typing – that most penetrating of sounds – would disturb Maurice.

'He rallies so often, but he's sinking every day. Still, his mind is very clear.'

They sat down and allowed the silence of the room to envelop them like a cloak on a cold day.

'You're worried about him, I think,' said Grace at last, suddenly changing her mind, as people so often do when they feel that they have been discreet too long. 'Is there anything that can be done about Maurice?' She rearranged the blue scarf about her neck. Both knew she was not talking about the dying man's health.

'I don't think so.' There was a finality about Jim's words and a heavy sadness in his expression which told Grace that at least he had tried.

'It's hard to understand these things.' Neither of them wanted to admit that it was Eddie they were now chiefly worried about. In spite of her tact and unfailing sympathy, Grace had all the childless woman's craving to arrange other people's lives according to her own lights.

'If one tries to understand them.' Jim looked at her steadily. 'Sometimes it's better not to try.'

She had a feeling that she was being left out of something which was more involved and delicate than Jim cared to discuss. She remembered The La's words and her own uneasiness about Eddie. She changed her tactics, hoping quite deliberately to kill two birds with the one stone.

'The bishop told me he called.' The blue scarf was taken off, folded carefully and without much reason on her lap. She seemed much concerned about it.

'The pair of you seem to be in great cahoots over me.' His

127

voice was stern but Grace, looking up from her silk prop, noticed that his face had softened. The bishop was much encouraged and she was glad that they had broken the ice at last.

'He was very concerned, always. I suppose he told you of his plans?'

'Yes. It was not what I expected, but you have to hand it to him, he's a great old warrior. He said he'd call again.'

'I hope you'll be able to help Eddie.' She was prodding her way gently. 'When all this is over. We'll all do what we can, of course. But I have a feeling he'll turn to you. If he doesn't I don't know what'll happen to him.'

Jim rose and walked to his desk with long nervous strides. She followed him closely with her eyes. Jim's face darkened and a strange antagonistic expression narrowed his eyes before he turned away. He leaned his knuckles on the desk and stared at the window.

'There is nothing I can do for Eddie,' he said harshly. 'He'll have to look after himself.'

'Oh Jim, you can't mean that.' She was shocked and sounded it.

He turned towards her with his back to the window so that she could not see his face with any great clarity. But she could sense that his whole body was tense and rigid as a coiled spring. Not for the first time did she realize that there was a side to this man's character – suppressed and controlled – which she would never understand. In spite of his dark Spanish good looks, his strong lean figure and his enormous physical vitality, she had always thought of Jim Dillingham as profoundly sacerdotal. Not sexless – but essentially intellectual and capable only of cerebral passion. She was a little confused as she often was with men.

'Will you be seeing Curley again?' he said sharply. 'Is he still in town?'

'Yes, he's in Dublin.' She relaxed. So this was it. She should have known that that encounter, after so many years, would affect Jim more than any other issue, even the fate of Maurice or Eddie's future.

He walked quickly into his bedroom, while Grace

knotted her scarf about her throat again. When he came back he was holding a small silver phial in his hands.

'Will you give him this and ask him to bless it, as he used to on Holy Thursday,' he said cryptically. 'He'll understand. I've replenished it from time to time, but I've never had the opportunity of having it blessed. If I have use for it, I'll do what I can for Eddie. Otherwise not.'

Grace stood up and put the phial in her bag. She did not know that it contained oil for chrisms and catechumens, and did not in the least understand what all this was about. But since it had something to do with the bishop she felt happy and content.

'Not that it might work out,' he said with a dry laugh. 'These things sometimes rebound on you, especially if you're not quite sure why you're doing it. But I'll take a chance because I suppose I want to.'

Grace looked at him questioningly but he was looking at the ground, biting his lip, his hands thrust deep in his pockets. She went out slightly puzzled and uneasy. The masculine mind had always seemed to her dark, mysterious and impenetrable – and never more so than now.

IX

Eddie received more for the snuff-box than he expected and became the object of more concern than he felt he deserved. Charles Williams, the art-dealer, gave him eight hundred and fifty pounds for it and assured him that he would make a hefty profit on it during the tourist season. It did not seem to him any great sacrifice to make at the time, since it helped to take his mind off the one inescapable fact which filled his thoughts, night and day. Greg's dumb and shame-faced gratitude when he pressed the money on him hardly touched him at all. He felt slightly embarrassed, aware that he was doing something which cost him very little. His reason, no less alert than it ever was, told him the gesture must appear almost unbelievable to Greg Hughes; and at another time this gift, which amounted to saving a family of friends from ruin, would have given him great pleasure. Now he was too numb emotionally to feel anything, and Greg too overwhelmed to say much. Yet this act, as is so often the case with generosity, was to have far-reaching repercussions, whether for good or ill he was never after-wards able to make up his mind.

It began with a phone call to the office from Dolly. She seemed more timid than ever, so that he could hardly hear her when she asked him if she might call and see him at home, and if he could arrange for Miss Keeley not to be present. At first he almost refused her: it meant half-an-hour away from Maurice and it occurred to him that it might be another excuse to get out of the house yet again. Greg told him that she had agreed to join a group of Alcoholics Anonymous and that a woman from the group was calling every evening to take her to a meeting, or sit with her when he was not there.

At half-six that evening he got rid of The La by telling her that he had to see a business contact who could not make it on time for the office. He hurried to the door and ushered Dolly into his room with a furtive glance at the back hall.

'I can't stay long,' she whispered, plucking at the belt of

her coat nervously, 'Liz is outside in the car, and I don't want to keep her waiting in the cold.'

Eddie had a vision of a hatchet-faced keeper of the wardress type counting the minutes that Dolly was out of her sight. And indeed the poor little creature did look as if she were a prisoner on parole: the same shabby appearance, the apologetic manner, the transparent pallor.

'I don't suppose it'll do her any harm,' he replied for want of something better to say. 'Sit down, Dolly, you look a bit tired.'

'I didn't know there were people like her in the world.' Dolly perched herself on the edge of the chair, and looked at him wonderingly with her great saucer eyes. 'You wouldn't believe all she'd done for me. There was once Greg rang her in the middle of the night and she came all the way from Monkstown. Of course she has a car – she's in the civil service – but all the same.' Her voice trailed off.

'You mean you like her?' Eddie's voice was equally wondering. He imagined Greg putting down his foot and taking strong measures, aided and abetted by the vigilant Liz. He could not help noticing Dolly's crushed appearance.

'Like her! I couldn't manage without her. And I'm not the only one she helps. Every minute she has off from work she spends with people like me.'

'How very kind.' He looked at his visitor with a slightly forced smile. Dolly was certainly taking her punishment gallantly.

'I don't know what would have happened to us,' he heard her say. 'God knows I didn't deserve what you did, but you don't know what it means to Greg and the children. If only there was something I could do.'

'Please, Dolly.' He attempted to laugh. 'You did me a good turn really. I'd never have got it back from Maria myself, and it was useless anyhow. It didn't cost me anything.'

'Oh, but – '

'Don't think about it, Dolly. I'm glad it was some use to someone.' He turned back, prepared for her brimming eyes.

131

He realized her need to express thanks, but wished very much that he did not have to listen to it. Apart from this natural diffidence, he sensed that there was something happening in the life of this faded, rather pathetic little woman which he would give a very great deal to have happen in his in a different way.

'So I had to see you to try and thank you, and promise – '

'Don't Dolly.' Eddie waved his hand in front of his face and closed his eyes. He heard her draw her breath with a start, and opened his eyes to find her staring at the door. Jim was standing there looking at them with a slightly startled air.

'Come in, come in,' said Eddie, glad of this interruption. He had warned off The La but neglected to tell Jim.

'Oh, Mr O'Connell,' cried Dolly, jumping to her feet, 'I'm that glad to see you looking so well again. I suppose you know what Mr Doyle has done for me. I can never thank him, and he's so decent he doesn't want to listen to me. If you only knew how good he is, and how much we appreciate that money. I'll never be able to thank him, but I'll always think of what he's done, and it'll always help me. I just want him to know, and I don't think I'd be able to say it if you hadn't come in.'

The words gushed out in that first confessional flood, which so often overcomes alcoholics at the beginning of their long, emotional struggle; a cross which, if they accept it, they must bear for the rest of their lives. Dolly was new to it and full of good resolutions, and would have exploded if she had not got what she wanted to say off her chest. Eddie hardly heard her in the shock of hearing Maurice's name and the embarrassment of having Jim confused with him.

Dolly too sensed that she had made a blunder as Jim stared at her perplexedly. For a few moments there was silence.

'I'm sorry,' said Jim, glancing at Eddie with a strange, penetrating look.

'Is anything wrong?' said Eddie quickly. 'Has anything happened?'

'No, no, I just dropped in. I didn't know there was anybody here.'

Dolly caught her breath and gave a little cry.

'This is Dolly Hughes, Jim, Greg's wife,' said Eddie helplessly. 'She just called in.'

'My name is Dillingham, Mrs Hughes.'

'Oh, my God! I was so full up I got all confused. But maybe you know about it too. I mean the snuff-box and everything?'

'Oh, that.' Jim chuckled. 'I suppose you brought it back.'

'You mean you don't know that Mr Doyle sold it,' burst out Dolly before Eddie could stop her. 'That's why I want to thank him. Greg doesn't know what to say. After he bringing it back and everything and the way I got rid of it.'

By now Jim had a fairly clear grasp of the situation in spite of Dolly's confused explanation. He attempted to cover up Eddie's embarrassment.

'It was very funny, really. I mean the way The La carried on,' he said lightly.

'Funny!' Dolly was not prepared for a light-hearted acceptance of anything. 'Oh, Mr Dillingham, may God forgive ye. Weren't we up to our eyes in debt, and didn't know what way to turn, only for Mr Doyle giving us the money for the gold box. I didn't even know how much we owed, I was in such a state, I was afraid to add up the bills. But now, thanks be to God, we're out of the wood, and it's all due to Mr Doyle. I'll never stop praying for him for the rest of my life. It's only when you're in trouble that ye find out what sort people are.'

'I tell you what,' cut in Eddie, 'I'll go out and see you some evening as soon as I can. I'd like to meet this Liz.'

'Oh sure, ye're welcome anytime. Only let me know in case there's a meeting, and I'll get Liz to stay with me instead. I told her how ye helped us, not everything of course, on account of Greg.'

'Of course, of course. I'd keep it to myself if I were you. And now I don't think you ought to keep Liz waiting in the cold too long.'

'Ye're not vexed with me or anything, are you Mr Doyle?

133

I mean for blurting it out in front of Mr Dillingham. I'm terrible sorry but I couldn't help meself, I'm that full up.'

Eddie took her arm and steered her towards the door, remembered The La and motioned her to remain while he looked out into the hall. Dolly took the opportunity of shaking hands with Jim, then with a quick impulsive gesture she kissed Eddie on the cheek, ran through the door and hurried down the steps into the night.

X

Eddie came back, holding his hand to his cheek, to find Jim poking the fire. When he straightened up after adding more coal Eddie knew from his expression that there was going to be some kind of confrontation. He went mechanically to the cabinet, poured himself a drink, and looked at his watch. Ten past seven. The nurse did not leave until eight.

'How much did you get for the snuff-box?' Jim sat down and crossed his long legs, pressing his forefingers together and tapping them against his chin.

'Oh what does it matter? Enough to pay their bills, or most of them. I wish we could buy our way as easily out of everything else.' Eddie, who felt cold, sat down on the hearth-rug and turned his back to the fire. With his legs crossed guru-wise, and his jacket hanging loose over his now slender frame, he looked young, and sad and remote.

'There are some things you can't buy your way out of, Eddie. All the same that was a very generous gesture. I think it shows you should try and do something more.'

One of the coals fizzled and a spark flew out over Eddie's shoulder and landed on the edge of the rug. Jim raised himself and stamped it out with his foot, while Eddie looked up at his dark intense face.

'What do you mean?'

'I didn't intend to say anything, or interfere. But this business tonight has made me think that maybe I ought to. Who knows what's behind all these things?' He settled back again, and unconsciously rested his arms on his chair with the long brown hands drooping over the edges.

'I don't mind what you say. It can't make a lot of difference now.' Eddie's voice was dull, and he did not seem much interested in the drink he held. He was staring at the tiny black speck where the live spark had been crushed into the rug.

'Perhaps not. But I've been talking to Maurice.'

Eddie squared his shoulders and looked round, suddenly

135

alert and interested.

'When?'

'The day he was brought home. He made his position quite clear. I think he had a feeling that I was trying to "get to him" as they say. Of course I wasn't. You can't force yourself on anybody like that. But he seems to be trying to reach out and live through you, in some kind of strange, tormented way. And it can't be done, Eddie. Not like that.'

Eddie turned his head and was staring at the door, his profile, marred by the slightly undershot lower lip, still and white as a marble bust. In all the years he had known him Jim had never seen him blush: when angry or agitated he became deathly pale. Now his skin was like waxed paper, and his thick brown lashes almost black by comparison.

'I don't believe that anybody who is capable of so much feeling as Maurice could reject everything so utterly, especially at a time like this.' Jim grasped the arms of his chair and stiffened his body as if he expected a blow. 'What he's asking you to do is hate everybody and everything, for him. And I can't believe he really means it. It isn't just that men brought up like him have some sort of hope bred in their bones – that applies to all sorts of people, Christian and otherwise. Even his rejection is against something positive, and that means he's fighting something in himself. But all that fades away when faced with this awful mystery, which even atheists respect. It's the one thing they can't explain, because death is not in man's nature.'

Eddie turned slowly and looked up, his slate-blue eyes thoughtful and probing. Jim always felt acutely uncomfortable when this mild-mannered man subjected him to one of his rare penetrating stares. He was well aware that Eddie possessed a subtle and formidable intelligence and an instinct which could be frightening, especially when he was not trying to be clever. Such mistakes as he made were nearly always the result of a heart continually at war with his intellect. This was proved by his failure to see through Dolly until she revealed herself, and even then he had apparently felt no animosity towards her for his own

136

blindness. Perhaps he was right. A genuine instinct for truth is never really deceived on the deepest level, and it was this element in Eddie's character that made Jim feel thoroughly uncomfortable now. There was nothing for it but to plough on, especially since the cross-legged figure remained silent, gripping his ankles with taut fingers.

'You would prefer to see him reconciled in some way, wouldn't you, Eddie? I don't mean in the conventional sense with bell, book and candle, but with himself.' Jim felt something stir and form in his mind as the hunched figure at his feet continued to stare at him. He did not understand what it was, but his body had grown cold and he wanted to reach out and touch something that was living, warm and vibrant. He would have held out his hand to Eddie if the other did not seem to be made of marble.

'Yes, of course I would,' said Eddie after what seemed a long silence. 'But I can't force him either.'

'I'm not talking about force. What he needs now is comfort, someone who'll show him that when it comes to this, we're all in the same boat. You can't love one person and hate everyone else. That isn't love, its possession.'

'Maybe it is.' Eddie's voice was quiet and unemotional. 'But that's the way he feels, and I can't let him down now.'

'He has a grudge and God knows I don't blame him,' Jim went on eagerly. 'But what he's rejecting, God or love or whatever you like to call it, is a caricature. I read about it someplace recently, and it put it just the way I've always wanted to put it. They reject this silly old man in the sky they've been taught to fear but they still look for love. And wherever you find it, no matter how or with whom, it's only part of something greater.'

'Love is indivisible?' There was a curious upward flick about Eddie's voice which made Jim look at him sharply, but the waxen face showed no change of expression.

'Well, isn't it? Wherever it's found, if it's true, there's some element of the divine about it and that includes everything and everybody. And it's the only thing we've got left when the grave is filled up. Other people and this element in them too.'

137

'I know that you've been reading,' said Eddie with a slight smile. 'The Dutch Catechism. I remember marking that passage. If you deliberately despise the greatest love, how can you arrive at an authentic love? It's impossible. It would end up as a collective lamentation.' Eddie paused and tapped his forehead, a habit he had when he was quoting. 'It goes like that, I think, or pretty near it. I remember looking it up when they asked me to review that book about Proust.'

In spite of his anxiety, or because of it, Eddie had managed to get two books reviewed in the past two weeks. He read at night, and knew exactly what he was going to say before he started to write it down. He got to his feet nimbly and crossed to the bookcase, took down a large volume in a red and white jacket, opened it and read out:

' "A dying person has nothing better to leave those around him than signs of his love and signs of his hope. And proofs of love and hope are also the last things that family and friends can provide for a dying man. Sometimes they can express these things in words; at other times merely through their faithful presence." '

He closed the book and put it back on the shelf, leaned his shoulder against it, crossed his feet, folded his arms over his chest and looked at Jim enigmatically.

'You know all the answers, Eddie. I thought you would.' Jim moved uneasily in his chair and stared down at his hands. He snatched them away from the chair arms and clasped them between his knees.

'If you can call them answers. Such as they are I agree with them. I'd even like to see the bell, book and candle, if you want to know.'

'Then how can you agree to this ...' Jim broke off, unable to express something which seemed to him demoniac.

'Have you ever been in love, Jim?' The question came, quiet and insistent and Jim now realized why he had felt so uneasy at the beginning of this interview. It had been an instinctive premonition of this very question. Eddie, as he expected him to do, struck back with unerring accuracy and left him defenceless. In spite of his genuine desire to help, and his real concern, Jim had made the old priestly blunder of handing out the old answers without committing himself. You do this and you do that; but do not ask me what I have done. It was the ultimate bland evasion.

He looked into the blazing fire and felt lost and helpless. One was supposed to see faces in flames but he saw nothing. He remembered two or three women in London; another in Paris; yet another in Vienna. They had been exciting, yes. He felt a heightened sensibility and once, the first time in London, came near to complete acceptance, until he discovered that he was merely one of many and must accept that if there was to be any future. She was quite honest about it, but that kind of love he could could not understand and would not accept. He considered that he had been unlucky, and once or twice the thought crossed his mind that this happens to people who do not really want to be involved. In any case he had never fully committed himself, and of that he was now bitterly conscious.

'I know that one doesn't have to suffer from a disease in order to prescribe a cure,' went on Eddie, quietly and inexorably. 'But that's different – the difference between science and religion. Science makes no moral claims. So before you start advising me on this particular subject, perhaps you'd better answer the question. I don't mean the crush you had on Grace. That was safe, even if you didn't think so at the time. But have you ever been totally committed to anybody?'

Jim swallowed his spittle and felt his throat dry. The two men he was talking about had not been afraid to commit themselves – and had kept their faith. What, when all was said and done, did he, Jim Dillingham know about it, in the name of Jesus?

'I'm sorry, Eddie.' He forced himself to look at this friendly enemy, fully aware that he could not conceal the shame and embarrassment in his eyes.

'You don't have to be.' Eddie crossed the room quickly and put his hand on his shoulder. It was all that Jim could do to prevent himself reaching up and grasping it. This at

139

least was some form of human contact, spontaneous and warm. The marble figure was flesh and blood after all.

'I don't want you to be disloyal,' went on Jim in a low voice after Eddie sat down on the sofa and waited quietly for him to recover himself. 'But you can't look at things the way Maurice wants you to, not all the rest of your life.'

'I can try. There isn't very much else left for me to do. But if what I've been reading out, and what you say is true, then I've failed anyway. The whole thing has just been a convenient arrangement. But I don't think it was. And after all it hasn't ended yet.'

'You mean you'll try and help him?'

Eddie raised his head, his heavy underjaw jutting a little.

'I'll do anything. I want him to have hope and some sort of acceptance of himself, because he'd be happier that way. But if he doesn't I'm not going to let him down.' There was a note of pride in his voice, of confidence too, and serenity. 'After all the catechisms could be wrong, you know. They have been before.'

Jim thought of what he had said to Grace, and remembered the oil of the sick which he had received that day from the bishop with a short note. He realized that he was falling back on an age-old symbolism, as a man who has lost faith in the doctors will often revert to quackery, a position which he did not know Eddie had also experienced in another way. What was the good of all this talk about love, if people did not act upon it? A saying of Augustine from his student days flashed through his mind. *Ama et fac quod vis.* Love, and do what you will.

Yet ashamed as he was, Jim made one last effort.

'I know I have no right to speak, Eddie. I only know that I don't want you to live under a shadow for the rest of your life. Even if Maurice does force this on you, can you be sure that you'll always feel as he does? You don't have that kind of bitterness. To carry this through you'd have to believe that he'd be with you always as he is now. And he won't. Surely at the bottom of his heart he must know?'

Eddie looked into the fire for a few moments, his face reflecting the dancing flames like glass. Presently he raised his head and looked at Jim's anxious eyes.

'If he loves me, and love is what you say it is – and I think it is – then something will happen. What it will be, I don't know. And even if nothing happens, it'll still make no difference. He won't be left without care and attention. That's all I can do.' He pressed his fists into the sofa and pushed himself to his feet.

'Do you pray now, Jim?' he said, looking down at the dark troubled face pointed towards him.

In spite of himself Jim felt himself redden. It was a long time since anybody had succeeded in making him do that and he wanted to come out with an obscenity.

'Yes, sometimes,' he mumbled.

'Well, do it now,' said Eddie starting for the door, looking at his watch. 'And while you're here, have a drink. I forgot to get one for you. It's nearly eight and I have to read the nurse's bulletin. She says I'm a dab hand at giving injections now.'

XI

The nurse had her hat and coat on when Eddie got to Maurice's room, out of breath from his quick dash upstairs. The old woman smiled and nodded, pointed to the dressing-table and said in her cracked, off-key voice, 'I've left the usual instructions. See you in the morning.' With a smile at Maurice who responded by lifting his hand from the eiderdown, she slipped out of the room and was gone.

'Have given the usual dose. Temperature a little higher. May be restless during the night. Injection at four a.m. In emergency ring 66519.' This he knew was Isaacson's private house and it was the first time he had indicated that he would be willing to come during the night. It was not his usual practice, except for private patients in a nursing-home and even then it was unusual, as the nurses were capable of handling most emergencies. The busy doctor was certainly proving himself a staunch ally.

'What does she say?' Maurice's voice was still strong, but now he rarely raised it above a murmur, as if he were conserving his strength.

'The usual.' Eddie put the note in his pocket and sat down on the chair vacated by the nurse. She had left a thriller behind her with a lurid cover entitled 'Blood on the Window-panes'. It was extraordinary the appetite gentle old ladies had for tales of violence and gore.

'Another injection?'

Eddie nodded. For the past few nights it had been necessary to give one at four in the morning. He had been too preoccupied with learning how to handle a syringe with steady hands and without flinching to inquire what it was he was administering. He had taken to dosing himself with codeine which made him sleepy and necessitated the use of an alarm clock, but so far he had managed well. Needs must. Now it occurred to him that he was giving a pain killer. Leukemia did not always end in an ultimate weakness and coma.

'Yes,' said Maurice, twisting his head from side to side on the pillow. 'They're trying to deaden it now. What time does she say?'

'Four.' How much was he suffering? Eddie thought with sudden alarm. Although he heard him groaning a few times during the night recently, he never complained.

'Make it three. That's the worst time. I've been looking through one of Mrs MacMaster's whodunits. Something about injecting air into the veins. It finishes you off in a few minutes. You wouldn't think of giving me that, would you? It would be nice and clean and save a lot of trouble.'

Eddie felt cold with fear. Nothing that Maurice had ever said filled him with such repulsion. The door of the front room was half open and he-could see the end of his own bed.

'Don't talk like that, Maurice. You know I couldn't do it!' He felt ashamed and inadequate as he stumbled over the words.

Maurice turned his head and looked at him, and Eddie felt that the glittering eyes were reading the hidden depths of hope and longing that he could not stifle.

'I didn't think you would, Eddie. It's a pity because I can't do it myself. You'd have to be a different sort of person, and I can't change that now.'

'I'd have to be a different sort from the beginning,' said Eddie with sudden inspiration. 'Would you have put up with me if I was?' Strange that he had never thought of this until now. Desperation often stumbles on unexpected explanations. Six months ago he would never have believed that he would be capable of handling a syringe: he whose hands trembled whenever he was agitated or excited.

The white pillow made Maurice's face even more yellow than it was, and his teeth when he drew his lips back in a smile gleamed as if they were false. Eddie had got used to the sickly sweet smell of the room, but he still flinched when the sick man attempted to smile.

'I suppose you're waiting for a miracle, you and Jim and the others. Grace, they used to call it when I was a nipper. I could never understand what it was, this grace, unless you wanted it. Then it comes pouring down. Well, of course. Self suggestion.'

'No, it doesn't.' The clutched straw seemed to be breaking in his hand, and Eddie went over to the bed. The hand he took in his was bony, hot and dry, but it did not draw away. Perhaps this was the only grace he would ever know.

'You were late tonight,' said Maurice, stroking his friend's wrist gently with his thumb. 'Had you a visitor?'

'Dolly.' He thought it better not to mention his talk with Jim.

'Oh, her. Is she still on the bottle?'

'No. She's given it up. Is it very difficult?'

'I forget.' Maurice dismissed Dolly with a slight shrug, but kept watching Eddie with his glassy stare. 'I told Jim that I had never accepted you,' he went on, slowly, tightening his grasp on Eddie's wrist. 'I didn't want him interfering, and I haven't changed in that. But it wasn't true what I said to him about you. I shouldn't have tried to change you. I think it's just that I can't bear to see you left alone.'

Eddie covered Maurice's large dry fist with his other hand and clung to it. He did not care if his eyes were wet with tears, or that his whole body was trembling with an effort to prevent himself breaking down. Yet at this final moment, which he felt in his heart was the farthest they would ever go in their long mutual journey, a weight had been lifted from him and he could find no words to say.

Bestowing it, Maurice did not feel the same need for reticence. He spoke on in a low calm voice, only his hand and his eyes expressing the trust and gratitude he was trying to express. In the end, although he did not think of it in that way, it was he who was giving absolution.

'I'm tired now and I can't say much. But I know you won't forget. I've been lucky. If you remember all this, remember it in your own way, and maybe someday it'll make sense to you.' He reached up his wasted arm and rested his other hand on Eddie's shoulder. 'This is the only sense I've ever been able to make of anything.' He drew the trembling figure with its tear-stained face down and pressed the head against his shrunken chest for a few moments. When he released him Eddie sat up and pressed his knuckles against his eyes like a child.

Presently he stood up and began to move about the room, rearranging everything which had already been put in place by Mrs MacMaster; picking up brushes, glasses, towels, jars and cushions, then putting them back more or less where he found them. He went into the front room, fetched his hot-water bottle, filled it from the tap in the wash-basin in the lavatory on the landing and put it into his bed. He set the clock for ten to three, picked up the book about Proust which he was finishing, flicked through a page and put it back on the night table. Then he went back to the sick room, sat down in the chair and looked at the figure in the bed. It was his habit to stay like this, talking if Maurice wanted to, or just simply staying with him until ten or half-ten, when he took his codeine, went to his own bed and tried to sleep after reading some of his book. But tonight there did not seem anything to say and the minutes ticked by precious and lost, like all things rare. It was Maurice who broke the silence.

'You might as well go to bed now. I'm sorry that I can't do what you want me to at the end. I know the way you'd like it to be. I know you'd like me to make some sign. But don't worry. Even if I go in my own way, remember I haven't forced it on you. You won't have to think of me like that, and you won't have to blame yourself for doing nothing. I can't share all that with you, but I don't want you to feel that you had to turn your back on it because of me.' He moved a little and held up his hand. Eddie got up, clasped the outstretched fingers, touched the hot forehead with his damp palm and went into his room, followed by the dark lingering glance of the dying man.

Eddie left the lamp on when he got into bed, but did not take up his book. So much had happened to him in this house. There were so many memories of that shared life, the secret of which had been so closely and jealously

145

guarded from the world. Speak low if you speak love. That had always been necessary for them. It heightened rather than diminished that physical union which even now Eddie did not regret. Without it, the complete sympathy they had achieved would never have been possible. But he did not dwell on that now. Instinctively he was storing it up for the future, when there would be no warmth, no protecting arms, no safe haven from the hostile world. In the end it was their trust, stripped to the bones of all things fleshy that survived. Neither had failed the other. It seemed to him now, as the silence enveloped him with its memories and its realities that theirs was a love as strong as death. Not having Jim's training, this made him think of Maupassant instead of the Song of Solomon. Surely this could be applied in its fullest sense to their relationship, for it implied a complete lack of sentimentality, an active acceptance and utter self-abandonment. They did not make use of each other, seeking only a reflection of self. Different as they were they kept their respect and in the end Maurice had set his friend free.

Once or twice Eddie thought he heard a low groan from the other room, and was on the point of going in but restrained himself for fear that he would give alarm. Eventually, strangely happy and almost content, he dozed but woke before the alarm. The light was still on on his night table. He looked at the alarm. It was one o'clock. He listened for a sound from the next room, but all was silence. Maurice was, no doubt, asleep. It occurred to him that he would slip in and sit with him for a while. He got up quietly, put on his dressing gown and slippers and opened the door softly. There was no light except the faint glow from his own reading lamp, and it took him a few minutes to grow accustomed to the semi-darkness. Then he became aware of a curious smell which he had never noticed before. He approached the bed and bent forward to listen to Maurice's breathing. But his head was not on the pillow, although he could make out the outline of his legs under the clothes. Had he reached out for something and slipped? Eddie moved his hand lightly over the sheets and stopped

146

dead, frozen with fright as he encountered something warm and sticky. He did not know how long it was before he tore himself away and ran to the switch, to face what he already half-suspected had happened.

Maurice was twisted round in the bed, the upper part of his body hanging over the side near the night-table. One hand lay thrown out behind him on the eiderdown. It was covered with blood; while the other rested on the carpet, limp as the neck and shoulders which lolled over the side of the bed. Both wrists were bleeding and a dark stain was already spreading over the worn green rug beside the night table. This was open and a razor lay on the ground in front of it.

Eddie did not cry out; but he lost his head; turned from the room blindly and ran down the stairs to Jim's flat. He burst in, switched on the light, dashed into the bedroom, shook the sleeping figure by the shoulder fiercely and silently. There was no need for him to explain anything. Jim was instantly awake when he saw the expression on Eddie's face. He jumped up and followed him upstairs, bare-footed and in his pyjamas.

Somehow they got the limp bleeding figure back into the bed, and Jim bent down and felt his chest.

'He's still alive. Get some bandages. He's slashed his wrists.'

'There aren't any,' stammered Eddie, unaware that in his horror he was clinging to Jim's arm.

'Then get a sheet and we'll tear it up. We may be able to stanch the flow. Hurry. Your own bed.'

Eddie ran into his room, pulled the sheet from the bed and began to cut it up with the scissors he kept on the table for paring his nails, stumbling as he hurried back snipping at the linen. Jim grabbed the sheet out of his hands, tore it into strips and began to bind the bleeding wrists tightly above the open scars. The whole operation took perhaps ten minutes, but to Eddie it seemed hours. When at last they settled him back on the pillows, Maurice's face was corpse-like but he was still breathing.

'The doctor will have to be called,' said Jim briskly,

hitching up his pyjama pants and tightening the cord.

'It'll be too late,' cried Eddie wildly. 'For God's sake give him absolution.'

'I can't do that,' said Jim sharply. 'He doesn't want it. It would be a mockery.'

'Oh for Christ's sake, what do you know about anything? He gave me a free hand tonight, took back everything he had made me promise. It was the last thing he said. This is his way of ending it. How do you know what's going on in his mind? Give it to him, I tell you, he always knew I wanted it that way.'

They stood for a few moments glaring at one another like murderous enemies. Eddie could think of nothing except Maurice's last words. A whole jumble of emotions which he could not express raced through his body as he made this appeal. Jim thought of the Ritual book which he kept with his breviary. He thought of the oil of the sick which the bishop had blessed for him. This man had repudiated all that. And yet ...

'He said he didn't want to change me. He knew what that meant. Will you ever understand anything? There may still be time. Give it him, I tell you. He tried to save me from watching him die without it. But why did I wake up? Why did this happen? He won't refuse anything I want. Go on, for the love of God, and forget yourself for once.' Eddie knelt down by the head of the bed and began to whisper the act of contrition into Maurice's ear.

Jim bowed his head at this rebuke, reminded of a Mystery he would never understand, and for the first time in many years raised his hand and was conscious of the power that was still in him. Eddie remained kneeling as the words, which Jim knew only in Latin, sounded quietly in the silent room. They came back to him, as if he had said them only yesterday.

'May the Almighty God have mercy on thee, and forgive thee thy sins, and bring thee to life everlasting. Amen. May the almighty and merciful Lord grant thee pardon, absolution and remission of thy sins. Amen. May our Lord Jesus Christ absolve thee: and I, by his authority, absolve thee from every bond of excommunication and interdict, so far as I can and thou hast need. Then, I absolve thee from thy sins, in the name of the Father, and of the Son and of the Holy Ghost. Amen. May the Passion of our Lord Jesus Christ, the merits of the Blessed Virgin Mary and of all the Saints, whatever good thou shalt have done and evil thou shalt have endured be to thee unto the forgiveness of sins, increase of grace, and the reward of life everlasting. Amen.'

It seemed to Eddie that the ghastly figure stirred, as if some remote fibre of his being was conscious of the words that had been said over so many of his ancestors, in good days, and in hurried furtive whispers during the long dark centuries. Jim opening his eyes, saw the movement and stopped. There were so many prayers to be said, but he felt impelled to say one more. The Sacrament was not in danger of being insulted. There was only himself, and the words he remembered so vividly. How many death beds had he recited this prayer over.

'Now go and ring the doctor,' said Eddie in a clear voice. 'And put on your dressing gown and slippers or you'll get your death of cold.'

When he was gone, Eddie drew up a chair and took one of the bandaged hands in his and pressed it gently. It seemed to him that there was a very slight response. This was a time when the soul was scraped. As he watched the sunken face and the wide staring eyes he was overcome by the memory of another death; his mother's. It had been very different from this. There had been candles, a crucifix, holy water, the ritual vessel with clean drinking water, and the finest linen cloth in the house. There had been Acts of Faith, Hope, Charity and Contrition. There had been Holy Communion. There had been the Anointing of the eyes, the ears, the nostrils, the mouth, the hands and the feet. There had been the Litany of the Saints. There had been the prayers for deliverance with their majestic Old Testament lamentations. And there had been the great commendation which always remained in Eddie's mind. Go forth, O Christian soul, out of this world, in the name of God the Father Almighty, Who created thee.

His mother had been fully conscious and had assisted at all the prayers, dying in the bosom of the family she loved, and hopeful of the resurrection she so firmly believed in. As he sat by this lonely bed, holding the hand of this beloved stranger whose innermost heart only God could read, he felt more aware of the awful mystery of death which has corrupted the nature of man, than he had experienced at his mother's passing. A holy death, they all had said, and so indeed it had been, sorrow tempered by the strength of a united and affectionate family. A gentle soul departed in a gentle fashion.

How very different was this tormented racking of soul from body. A man, delivered over for most of his life to what the world called vice, who ended his life in solitude and in a way which many would consider more terrible than his life. This was something that really called for mercy beyond the mystery. Eddie pressed the hand in his and gave a little cry as he felt it returned. The dark eyes slowly turned and looked into his, and all his life afterwards he believed he saw peace in their hidden depths.

XII

Maurice died an hour after Dr Isaacson arrived. Officially it was of course a case of suicide, but here again they were saved from endless embarrassment by that personal inter-pretation of the law which is instinctive to Irishmen and beyond the understanding of the English. Max Isaacson was a Jew and a Zionist, and had that cautious respect for law and order inherent in all minorities. But he was also an Irishman and he knew that his fellow countrymen, whose temperament was so closely akin to the international race to which he also belonged, believed in a decent discretion in matters which might give public scandal. The number of suicides in Dublin was no less than those in other cities of comparable size, but they were rarely published. Families and friends had to be taken into account and, in the last resort, who could judge of such matters? Maurice would have died in a week or two in any case. How he would face his Maker was not the doctor's concern. One look at Eddie, Jim and The La, roused from sleep and clad in a pink velvet dressing gown with a worn marabout collar, was enough to convince him that the letter of the law was out of the question. He wrote out a certificate of death resulting from acute leukemia, and went off in search of Mrs MacMaster who would believe what she read, and was experienced in the washing and laying out of corpses.

The La reverted to type, as she always did in moments of crisis. She made tea. Eddie refused to budge from Maurice's bedside and Jim in spite of some concern went downstairs with her, intending to bring up a tray before the nurse arrived.

'How did he do it?' was The La's first question after she had put the kettle on the ring in her tiny kitchenette and rejoined Jim in her sitting room.

'With the razor the nurse shaved him with. She used to leave it in the drawer of the night table, with the brush and the shaving cream. I suppose she should have kept it in the bathroom, but since she had to shave him in bed, it was

151

handy. Besides how was she to know a thing like that would happen?' Jim had dressed and lighted a fire in Maria's grate, but he felt chilled and drained. Before the doctor arrived he and Eddie managed to change the top sheet of Maurice's bed, remove the eiderdown and the bedside rug, bundle the remains of Eddie's torn sheet along with them in a drawer, clean the razor and generally tidy up the room. It was a harrowing experience, especially since Maurice was still alive. Only then did they waken The La, Jim telling her what had happened. He knew it would be impossible to keep it from her, particularly with the nurse and doctor arriving. And he felt the need to tell someone. Maria had risen to the occasion superbly; gone to the room, fell on her knees and blessed herself, then took Eddie in her arms. He sobbed like a child on her shoulder, silently and quietly, while she stroked his head and rocked him to and fro gently as if he had been the son she never had.

'May the Lord have mercy on his soul, the unfortunate creature,' she said now, surrounded by the momentoes of her colourful past, her tear-stained face puffy and pale, unaware of her sagging body and dishevelled wisps of dyed hair. With an ear cocked for the boiling of the kettle she gave Jim a sharp look. 'Did you anoint him?' Her voice was imperious: not the arrogance of the opera singer, but the realistic insistence of the old peasant woman who knows what things to put first. It would be a very foolish man who would leave this world without his passport signed.

'No.' Jim shivered as he crouched over the fire. 'There wasn't time. But I gave him absolution.'

'And the Act of Contrition?' The pugnacious jaw that had been lifted against many a claque in Milan and Vienna was thrust defiantly forward.

'Eddie said it in his ear.'

'Did he know?'

'I hope so.'

'Eddie wouldn't do it otherwise. You may be sure of that.' The kettle hissed and she hurried out, while Jim covered his face with his hands, pressing his nails into the flesh as if he wanted to prove to himself that he was still capable of feeling.

'How do you know that?' he asked when she came back with the teapot.

'I know.' The La's voice was mysterious. 'You told me how Eddie woke up. What woke him? I was afraid of my life that that poor unfortunate that's gone to God would force Eddie to keep you or any other priest out of the room until it was too late. And he would too. But look how it turned out. Thanks be to God and His Blessed Mother this night. You may be sure it was the Madonna who woke that poor boy in the night. Here, take your tea, you look famished. God's ways are strange. And now we'll have to get a clean sheet for the bed and lay him out proper.'

She sat down and watched him while he gulped his tea with shaking hands. In her eyes there was a strange look, half jubilant, half shrewd, and Jim wondered at this curious mixture of practicality and mysticism; not less since he had heard it often long ago. The La, like so many of her kind, was determined to plant the most unlikely souls in the hands of God. And who was to say she was wrong?

'And the habit!' she exclaimed. 'He'll have to be laid out in a habit. What would his mother think if he was laid in his coffin in a night-shirt or a pair of pyjamas, like a heathen. She'd turn in her grave.'

'But we haven't one,' protested Jim weakly, spilling tea into his saucer.

'Oh, yes we have. I have mine in a drawer inside. Third Order habit that I had blessed by Padre Pio. I was keeping it for myself, but sure I can get another any day blessed in Adam and Eve's. I'll get it this minute. And I have a small crucifix too to put in his hand, blessed by Pope Pius, the one who died the year of the war. Isn't it a wonderful thing that that poor man who thought he was an atheist, the Lord save us, would live to be togged out in a habit blessed by a saint that had the blood pouring out of his hands every Friday, and a cross blessed by the pope who canonised the Little Flower. I'll get it now, or Mrs MacMaster won't

153

know what to do. She'll think we're all a bunch of pagans. Amn't I glad I have it! Sure I don't grudge it to him at all. When all is said and done I'm fairly well fixed up, even if I drop dead in the street tomorrow, but poor Maurice has more use for a holy habit than the likes of me.'

She disappeared into her bedroom and reappeared a few minutes later with a brown habit, neatly folded and smelling strongly of camphor, the small black crucifix, over which Pius XI had made the sign of the cross, neatly placed on top of the bundle. Jim had known several old ladies in his mission days who washed their shrouds every Monday and hung them out to air; an edifying sight for the neighbours. But he had not expected such foresight from The La.

He got up and was lifting the tray when Maria laid her hand on his arm.

'The gloves,' she said with a half groan. 'We must have white cotton gloves to lay him out decent. And besides they'll cover the bandages on his poor wrists. But look at the size of his hands. Mine wouldn't go on his thumb.'

'The habit will cover his wrists,' said Jim, thinking that Eddie's tea would be pretty strong by the time he got it up to him. 'And everybody doesn't use gloves.'

'Here,' went on The La, picking up a bottle of whiskey from the chest and putting it on the tray, 'He'll need a drop of that in his tea. And as for gloves, don't tell me that any respectable corpse was ever laid out properly without them. It was always the custom in my parish at home and you may be sure they have the same ways in Maurice's place. They do it in Italy too, in some places. I always thought it a lovely finishing touch. Don't you know that gloves are the sign of gentility and in the sight of God we're all equal? Besides they're nice to look at if the hands turn blue as they often do. Shocking, and he holding the Pope's crucifix. He'll have to wear them if only for that.'

'But where are we going to get them?' said Jim, making for the door.

'From the undertaker, of course. They always keep a stock of them, even in this benighted city. We'll have to ring and make arrangements first thing in the morning, and get them over here before Grace and Desmond arrive. He might be a bit stiff in the morning, but we'll get them on. You don't want the visitors to be shocked, do you?'

By the time he reached the hall, Jim was feeling slightly bemused. Yet he knew there was an ancient wisdom in these arrangements, apart from their symbolism. In Ireland grief always comes later and is never forgotten. During the laying out, the waking and the coffining there is plenty to occupy the mind. The La left her bundle on the hall table, explaining that she would leave it there until the nurse arrived, when they would have to get Eddie down to his own flat while the women's business of washing and clothing the remains was carried out according to protocol. The La clearly intended to help Mrs MacMaster here.

'It's years since I laid out a corpse,' she said calmly, drawing her pink dressing gown about her regally. 'A neighbour he was, an old bachelor of ninety-eight who could remember the famine. Sure he wasn't the size of a monkey-nut. Now about the arrangements ...'

They were interrupted by the arrival of the nurse who had been left at the door by Dr Isaacson. She came in with a sinister looking little black box, to be warmly embraced and kissed on both cheeks by The La, who then swept her upstairs, ordering Jim to stay behind and make fresh tea for Eddie.

Jim stood in the hall, holding the tray, until he saw Eddie coming down, pale as chalk, but fully dressed and with his hair neatly brushed. They went down to the flat, drank tea laced with whiskey and sat by the fire for what seemed an age. The only thing either of them ever remembered about that interval was the cuckoo-clock striking five. A few minutes afterwards The La swept in, ordered more tea with spirits for Mrs MacMaster, and disappeared into her bedroom to dress. Jim made the tea and had gone up when she reappeared, arrayed in black silk and wearing a gold chain and cross about her neck.

'Now about the arrangements,' she said, sitting down beside Eddie on the Moroccan hassock and taking his

155

hand. 'You know his home address, don't you?'

Eddie nodded.

'He has a brother in the home place, hasn't he? Well he'll have to be told. No matter what Maurice might say, I'm sure he'd want to be buried with his own people. I'm sure they have a plot, the neighbours will dig it, if only to make sure that they get their own dug in return, and he'll be back with his own which is what we all want. Besides, the price of plots in Dublin is outrageous.'

Eddie assented with another nod. What did it all matter now? He did not know that The La, apart from her very real feeling about returning the dead to their own, was also anxious that there would be no scandal about burying Maurice in Dublin and Eddie demanding to be buried with him when his time came. Eddie was also ear-marked for the family plot.

'Then there's the Mass. I suppose we'd better leave that to Grace. If she doesn't know the parish priest, she'll be bound to know someone who does. I wouldn't be at all surprised if they said High Mass in a place like that in Latin, which will be nice to hear again. I can't stand this vernacular stuff. It's like opera in English. Have you enough tea? Here, I'll freshen it up. You have enough whiskey on an empty stomach. Ah Jim.'

She turned as he came in, and pointed to the chair where he obediently seated himself to await further instructions. 'Now, first thing in the morning you'll have to take that certificate round to the Register and have it fixed, I mean recorded. Otherwise it won't be in order. Are you listening to me? I'll get on to the undertaker, a very nice man from my own part of the country, who lives in Kimmage. He'll charge no fancy prices to me and I'll get him to send the gloves over here the minute he opens.'

'Oh, the gloves,' said Eddie, coming out of his numbed trance with sudden interest. 'Like my parents had. I never thought of that. We must have them.'

'Of course.' The La gave Jim a look of admonishment. 'Now about the coffin. Would you like purple handles? I always fancied them myself. Right then, we'll have them.

156

Oh yes, I almost forgot. I'll have to get white socks as well as gloves. Jim, go and put on the kettle. Now, is there anything else?'

'Are we all going to go?' said Eddie, looking at her anxiously.

'Glory be to God!' The La's voice was indignant. 'You don't think we're going to let him go back without a friend following him. You have your car, which Jim can drive, and I'll go with you. Desmond and Grace have theirs. And I have no doubt some of the people from the shop will want to go. And the Hugheses. Somebody will give them a lift.' She broke off and looked at her Florentine chest. She sighed and blessed herself, while Jim and Eddie looked at her blankly.

'And to think only a week ago, or was it two? I was threatening to have that woman arrested for making off with my Orsini snuff-box. But sure isn't it all one in the end? It'd be in it after me. If that poor creature wants to come in and say a decade of the Rosary for them that's gone, I won't pretend I noticed a thing.'

XIII

The only business which can be expedited in Ireland with complete and absolute efficiency is a funeral arrangement. No matter how remote the place of burial or how scattered the relatives, the word goes forth with magical potency, and the mourners, the undertaker and the priests gather swift as swallows at the first approach of autumn.

By half-past ten that morning the gloves and socks had been delivered, and the coffin and hearse promised for three o'clock for its long journey across the country. Grace, contacted by telephone, went to work immediately. She rang the parish priest of her native town who knew the parish priest of Maurice's townland. Half-an-hour afterwards he rang back to say that the brother had been contacted, the grave was being opened and the curate would be at the church at seven that evening to receive the remains. The Requiem Mass would be said at eleven the following morning and the funeral would take place immediately afterwards.

At noon the visitors began to arrive: Grace and Desmond, who stayed on to be with Eddie; the staff from the shop, singly and in pairs came with their Mass cards; and lastly Greg and Dolly who was the first to sound an echo of the ancient Irish caoine, the wailing lament that lies so close to the heart of every Irish woman. She fell on her knees at the end of the bed and burst into loud and bitter tears. The La, who was sitting by the pillow, carefully keeping the custom that the body should never be left alone for an instant from the moment of death to its committal to the earth, made no effort to silence her. Greg slipped his arm about his wife's shoulders, awkwardly since he knelt, old-style, on one knee.

Maria Keeley felt strangely comforted as she raised her Rosary beads to her lips, kissed the cross and blessed herself. She had seen to the proprieties. Fresh linen sheets of the best quality had been found for the bed; a fine napkin covered the night-table and on it she had placed a lighted candle (65% wax) and a vessel of holy water with a sprinkler. She insisted that all the clocks in the house be stopped according to immemorial custom, and the mirrors on the dressing table and in the wardrobe, symbols of earthly vanity, decently covered. She earmarked one of Maurice's suits to give to his brother so that he could wear it to Mass for at least three Sundays after the burial. The rest, after Eddie and Jim had taken whatever memento they wished, must be given to the poor. All this she had done; and even Grace could see that every proper respect was paid to one who in death had passed beyond the highest of human aspirations.

But as yet, apart from the silent tears which Eddie had shed on her shoulder, no one had wept openly for Maurice, and without that no final parting was complete.

Dolly, as she sobbed brokenly, her thin shoulder pressed against her husband's side, was not merely weeping out of pity and sorrow for a man she hardly knew who had gone to an untimely reckoning. She wept, as most people do when confronted with the awful majesty of death, for all mortal things, for hopes that fade and bright promises that are unfulfilled, for all the griefs and disappointments of life, for the sure knowledge that everything loved and cherished must one day dissolve into dust. But most of all she wept for herself; for the pain she had given to the embarrassed man who was now sheltering her with his arm, for the wrong she had done to her children, for all the dreams she once had and could no longer even remember. For the subtle, inexorable erosion of life.

In his brown habit, with his gloved hands holding the crucifix and folded peacefully across his breast, Maurice looked like an image of some medieval conquistador: the long, high arched nose, jutting from the emaciated face, the wide mouth set in a grim enigmatic smile, the huge eyes closed and sunken in mystery.

'Oh,' said Dolly, stifling her sobs as she sprinkled holy water over his body, 'did you ever see such a lovely corpse. He's like a statue in the church. May the Lord be good to him and have mercy on us all.'

159

The La kissed her on the cheek, and Dolly who had certainly not expected to be attacked for her misdemeanour in a house of death, but was unprepared for this, burst into renewed weeping and had to be led from the room firmly, on Greg's arm. After a few awkward but painfully sympathetic words with Eddie in his flat, where they met Desmond and Grace and the managing director of the firm for whom Maurice worked, they went away promising to attend the funeral. Greg had already arranged for the loan of a car from a colleague and taken a day off.

Shortly before the undertakers arrived, they all went to take their final leave of the man who had so strangely touched their lives. They kissed his forehead and made the sign of the cross on it with their thumbs, and Eddie looked upon the face of his friend for the last time with a simple restrained tenderness which moved even Desmond, who hated illness, death and funerals in a most unIrish fashion.

It was a long journey west and a cold day. As they passed Leixlip, Eddie thought of his father and the first breath of home. A high glassy sky and a brittle sun shone down on the muted fields. The little towns and villages slipped by; Maynooth, Kilcock, Enfield, Kinnegad, Milltownpass, Rochfortbridge, Tyrrellspass, Kilbeggan, Moate, all garishly painted in Tourist Board colours. The mountains melted away behind them and the long low rim of the horizon spread out unendingly before them, as elusive as the quiet land through which they passed. Here all was flat or gently undulating, silent and wide open to the limitless sky. Yet it had an air of secretiveness, a kind of slumbering watchfulness with which they were all familiar.

Maurice was born not more than twenty miles from the town in which Eddie and Grace were raised, and in which Jim once ministered. When he caught his first glimpse of its roofs and spires, naked to the sky and purple against the sinking sun, Eddie began to talk in a bright unnatural manner. The narrow streets, the great span of river, the near presence of his old home held too many memories for him to indulge them now. The most painful memory of all; that of childhood, when the heart is unaware of its own tortuous seeds, which blossom so strangely with the years and are still in the root when the leaves drop dead.

This was not a time for revisiting those scenes. That was another life, a different country and Grace, with her usual tact, had not informed Eddie's brother. It was not necessary for her to tell him of this. He understood. This time they would not be stopping off, as they had done so gaily in the past.

Jim was silent most of the way as he drove. After the numbness and mechanical reactions of the night, he felt a growing sense of unease and a positive irritation as they neared the town. He gripped the wheel and looked neither to left nor right. He had often thought of this place with a certain nostalgia, especially during the past year, but now that he was confronted with it, he was overcome with something like physical nausea. All of them had their own reasons for keeping silent as they passed through it: Maria out of tact, Eddie for fear of breaking down. But Jim's reaction was the most violent, although he did not know it. A sort of black, poisonous anger filled his heart as he passed the church where he had once said Mass.

Nor did the feeling slacken as they drove further west into Roscommon, while the twilight deepened about them. He knew then, when it was too late, that he did not want to go through with this. As they drew near their destination, small knots of men at cross-roads lifted their hats as the cortège passed. The simple, courteous salute irritated him, while it touched Eddie and filled The La with pride in her own people.

But when, at the end of a long narrow winding road, they sighted the lighted chapel upon a hill, its steeple plume-black against the last long thumb of reddened horizon, he knew definitely that this was a place he did not want to enter. Nothing had changed and he knew exactly what to expect. A dozen cars were waiting in front of the gates. Four men stepped forward as the hearse drew up, all tall, burly, and bearing a vague resemblance to one another. The brother was immediately recognizable: a rougher, redder-faced, weather-beaten version of Maurice. The La congratulated herself. Her instinct had not deserted her. This man would fit the suit she was carrying as if it were made for him. But Jim narrowed his eyes at the sight of the priest in the lighted porch, throwing a long familiar shadow down the steps. The coffin was slid out of the hearse, hoisted on the shoulders of the brother and cousins, and Maurice was handed back to his own.

Part Three

I

'Patrick, do you believe that people get the things they want in life, if they really want them?'

'Yes, but not always in exactly the way they want them.'

The question was asked in a drowsy voice which did not conceal an undertone of anxiety and answered in a tone equally sleepy, but off-hand, even careless. Kate Vale turned her head and looked at the window with half-closed eyes. The holland blind was drawn and the blazing June sunlight outside gave it the appearance of a glowing slab of honey-coloured marble. The two naked bodies on the bed were suffused in a golden aureole which imparted some tint of life even to the man's banana-white skin, and turned Kate's own carefully acquired tan into a deep chocolate. With her thick black hair, full lips and slightly flat nose she looked a little like an Arab woman.

'Shall I light another?' she asked, looking at the four stubbed out butts on the ashtray on the night table.

'Half-past five. Time to move.' He was already sitting up, running his fingers through his long, silken blond hair. His small delicate features were as expressionless as ever as he swung his thin legs over the side of the bed and looked back at her. Kate lit a joint for herself and inhaled deeply to damp down the irritation which his casual matter-of-factness so often induced in her.

He stood up, straightened his tall slim body, and stretched his arms languidly. She opened her eyes. Now he was leaning against the door and was smiling with one corner of his wide pink lips.

'I think I'll call this my dish room,' he was saying with a little chuckle.

'Your what?'

He made a gesture which was intended to indicate the walls of the room. Painted a deep chrome yellow, every available space above table level was covered with china plates. Japanese, Korean, Chinese and French, the designs were varied and exotic, possessing one characteristic in common: they were all blue. But she had little sense of humour. She remembered only that some of them were priceless, got together by his grandfather and brought up from his house in the country.

'Oh yes, yes,' she went on hurriedly, getting off the bed. 'They go beautifully with the carpet.' She looked down at her feet and rubbed the worn pile with her toes, vaguely admiring its delicate blue and yellow shades.

'Throw something on. I think we should open that window. Desmond has old-fashioned ideas about dope.'

She looked round at the drawn blind angrily, but before she could speak she found herself in a flood of light, trapped and exposed, which made her cover her breasts with an involuntary gesture. He opened the door leading to the front room and the sun still high in the heavens was pouring through the two windows overlooking the square.

She put her rolled cigarette down on the ashtray and threw her clothes on quickly. As she pulled up the zip of her ready-made caftan and slipped her feet into her sandals, she could hear him pulling down the blinds in the other room. And then she could not find her belt. She called out to him and he came back to the door, the chain belt of imitation silver dangling from one hand, the other held up with the forefinger in front of his pursed mouth.

'Ssh. Don't scream. You left it out here.' He closed the door quietly and left her alone, taking the belt with him. She pulled up the blind and opened the window, leaning on the sill until she finished her joint, while she blew smoke defiantly at the blue sky and the roofs of the mews cottages facing on to Lad Lane, once a haunt of prostitutes and now as respectable as the Court of St James.

When she went into the next room time had begun to stretch a little, and it seemed to her she had absented herself long enough to justify something, exactly what she was not quite sure. She wanted to smoke some more but she knew he would not allow that. He was sitting at his desk copying a passage from an old tattered volume propped against a pile of similar books beside him. With scrupulous regularity he completed a thousand words a day in his neat hand which she afterwards typed out for him at home. On the rare occasions when his quota was not completed by the time she called, he always managed to polish it off before she left. It was not really carelessness or lack of industry but always a loose end which he knew he could tie up by copying a passage from one of his 'sources'. She realized with a dim pang that he had already made good use of her absence by the window.

'What a lot of scribblers there are in this house,' she said waspishly.

He finished a sentence before he answered her in his deep slow voice.

'Only two at the moment, Doyle and myself. Dillingham's correcting proofs.'

'What's the difference?' she scoffed, looking at the neat pile of typed manuscript at the end of the desk. Her own work. When the first draft was finished, he would revise it, and the whole damned thing would have to be retyped. There were times when she made up her mind that it was not worth it: but that was only when she was with him.

'This was the husband's flat, wasn't it?' She looked about at the 18th-century paintings of his family house, the old French chairs, the glass-fronted book-case with hand-cut panes that winked like diamonds, the comfortable studded wing chair by the fireplace.

'You told me it was an absolute shambles when you came here. And there was some story about his people descending on the place after he was buried and accusing the little wife downstairs of selling all his furniture, as well as making away with his money. Apparently they couldn't believe he hadn't more than the few sticks they found here.'

'So Desmond told me.' He was looking at her with his blank marble-eyed stare.

'Well, the little Doyle piece looks as if he's consoled himself pretty well since. He has that sleek look. I suppose the ex-priest has taken over. Pity, really. I know one or two girls who couldn't object to showing Dillingham the light. Very attractive, I think.' She was about to add 'don't you?' but his silent stare cut her off.

'I have no idea what's going on between them,' he said coldly, turning his completed page on to the blotting-pad and pressing it lightly with his clenched fist. 'It's none of my business.' His tone implied that it was none of hers either.

'I thought you couldn't stand the sight of them,' she demanded.

'One can't live in the same house with people and not get to know them a little. Not in Dublin anyway, even if we all have separate flats. Besides they're friends of Desmond's.'

'Dublin,' she said lightly. 'I'll never get used to it. It's worse than a small town at home.'

'Why should you? You're English. This is foreign territory.'

'I forgot what a Green Man you were,' she laughed. It still sometimes struck her as incongruous that an Anglo-Irish lordling, claiming to be a Republican, a socialist and an atheist, should be engaged on a biography of Lord Palmerston. His great-great-grandmother had been a relative of the Prime Minister's wife. They had dozens of letters from her and several from the old shit himself (Kate always called him that). The project was designed to reveal the subject, warts and all, and the letters to give it a touch of originality.

'I don't see why one has to be a hide-bound Tory to write about old "cupid",' he remarked, keeping to his main interest. 'If I were, I should probably try to white-wash him. As it is I can be objective. Even Doyle has to admit that.'

'What does that little queen know about it?' she rounded on him, buckling her belt.

'Nothing much. I was merely talking to him about it. After all, he's quite a clever critic.' He gathered the four hand-written pages together and levelled them neatly against the top of the desk. As the edge of the manuscript rapped against the wood she had one of her flashes of insight. He was getting the pair below to help him. That was why it had to be typed as it went along, so that he could show it to the prize pair in the flats beneath and utilize whatever suggestions they might make. The ex-priest, she believed, was quite famous in his own line and his boy friend was making a name for himself as a critic. Christ, she thought, as she looked down at the lean capable hands folding up the pages, is there anything or anybody that isn't grist to his fucking mill?

'Sure he wasn't making a pass at you?'

He gave her a cold appraising stare.

'I can see he's made quite an impression on you.'

He made no reply. Instead he began to smile, that slow, lop-sided and, to her, completely irresistible grin which always ended in a chuckle, and which seemed to take most of those who received the benefit of it – and especially his women – completely into his confidence. She forgot her own sense of being exploited in the assumption that she was sharing in the exploitation of others.

'Patrick,' she said fondly, stroking his long silken hair, 'you are the most awful shit.'

II

'Whew!' Eddie blew out his cheeks in mock relief as he laid down the proof-copy on a side table and shook his head. 'Thank God that's over. It's an awful bloody job.'

Jim, who was pouring drinks said nothing. It was lucky he was not given to after-thoughts. His original manuscript had been neatly and carefully typed: there was little to do with the proofs except correct printers' errors and check the punctuation. Eddie, who had a feeling for such things, insisted on going through it sentence by sentence, in the course of which he discovered that Jim was no longer even remotely involved with the book. He had heard of authors losing interesting when they completed something, but Jim seemed actually to dislike what he had written. Eddie felt he knew the reason why and asked no questions. It was one of the many unspoken thoughts which they shared.

'And to think that on top of all that, I have to run over Paddy Bellington's manuscript,' he said with a slightly forced gaiety as he took his drink, and sat down by the empty fireplace.

'You might be doing worse,' said Jim quietly.

Eddie looked up sharply, prepared to glance away again quickly. Jim was still standing looking out through the window, apparently staring at nothing. There was little in his voice or face to indicate that he meant anything other than he had said. But recently so much of what they said, even the most trivial remarks, seemed to imply many hidden meanings. Or so it appeared to Eddie. He stirred uneasily and sipped his drink as Jim went over to the other chair and stretched out his legs.

Jim leaned his head on the back of the chair and looked up at the ceiling. He was in his shirt sleeves, and his chest stretched the thin blue cotton, while black hairs glistened above his open collar. In the tawny heat of the room both of them could smell their own sweat. It was Saturday and they had been working all afternoon. Otherwise, Eddie had a feeling that the proofs would never get corrected.

'She's a junkie.'

Jim sat up and raised his eyebrows. Afterwards he was to remember this moment. A knot unravelled: the beginning of many things. Outside, although the tops of the windows were lowered, there was a momentary silence. The smell of the whiskey in his hand was faint but insistent.. Quiet and a certain easing of tension. A lock of hair was glued in the centre of Eddie's forehead, and little beads of sweat glistened on his upper lip.

'I knew they smoked pot but I didn't know they went farther than that.'

'He doesn't.' Eddie went on. 'He keeps to marijuana – and not much of that either. Catch him allowing himself to muck up things in the middle of a money-making project. Or at any other time either. But she's hooked. I don't think she's told him. If she had, he'd kick her out.'

'And what about his wife?'

'She runs the farm and the chickens and that great big castle they have in Tipperary. Paddy's father gave it to him to live in, but very little money. The whole family are as mean as cats' meat. The old man as you know lives in England. He writes books too – for money. Big glossy productions that sell like hot cross buns. So Paddy's cashing in on the racket.' It was something to talk about.

'With your help.' Jim stretched one arm and smiled.

'I correct the prose, which is awful. So far as I know, he's done his work fairly thoroughly but he can't write for toffee. Not that it matters. He'll have a big publicity campaign in all the glossy magazines and Sunday supplements. Paddy with wife and three kids on the steps of the castle complete with Labradors. Paddy close-up, modelling a suede suit and shirt. Paddy outside the door here to give the Georgian touch. The full treatment.'

Jim could not help looking at the proof-sheets of his own book and Eddie caught his glance.

'That's different,' he said unnecessarily.

Jim shook his head, but not in disagreement. He knew how it was. Eddie was new to the publishing world. Paddy's talk of publishers, editors, agents and foreign rights had got the better of his judgement. When he had written a few books of his own, and Jim had a feeling that he would, he would not be so romantic about it. But at the moment any new interest was better than time on his hands. And Jim knew only too well how he was spending that.

'You're too soft-hearted,' he said, attempting to gloss over a lot of things.

'Am I?'

Jim looked at the proofs of his book again and knew that it was probably the last one he would ever write. He realized now that apart from the financial necessity, his writing had been a substitute for the emptiness of his life. He had been numb and now was alive as never before. But he divined that the agony, the wild thrashing about in a vacuum which is more often than not a refusal to accept the ultimate loneliness of decision, was precisely the situation in which Eddie now found himself.

For some weeks after Maurice's death Eddie had been hardly more than half alive. He worked longer hours at the office, ate less and drank more. The La and Jim, coming into his flat in the evening to try and cheer him up, would find him staring into space with a book on his lap. Grace called every other day and had long worried consultations with Maria about him. In a month he lost a stone in weight. The descent of Maurice's relatives, all set to kick up a row, had been more of a relief than otherwise. They had taken every movable he possessed, but retired defeated on the money question since there wasn't any.

One evening, a week before Paddy moved in, Jim, coming out of his room to go down to Eddie, saw him going upstairs to the empty flat. He waited for a few minutes before going down to wait for him. It was a long wait and during it, Jim became aware that something strange was happening: a ghost was being exorcised and not only for Eddie. When at last he came back, Jim knew at once that the numbness had passed, knew also that his own vigils had not been mere acts of charity on behalf of a friend in need of support.

172

The restraint they had exercised in Maurice's lifetime had been a very real and necessary one.

Eddie was very pale and haggard when he came down from Maurice's rooms for the last time that evening. His expression of thankfulness when he read the concern in Jim's face was not forced. It was a time of unspoken gratitude and for Jim it was something more. Long restraint and the exigency of caution had not withered his emotions. He was strengthened and made a little reckless, awkward also in his attempt to break down the last barrier which would commit him to something dangerous and irrevocable. He stretched out his hand and Eddie had taken it and, in doing so, gently but firmly repulsed him.

At the time Eddie acted instinctively but afterwards it seemed to him to be an act of wisdom. Love is secret and moves mysteriously, even when it can be proclaimed to the world. The passion, complete, demanding and inevitable which existed between Maurice and the friend who was left to mourn him, was as rare as it was in its own way noble, and it came at the end of a long patient search for mutual identity. That which Jim offered was very largely the result of circumstance. All this Eddie knew at the time with his body and afterwards formulated in his mind.

And he was proved right. Jim's heart, so long closed to any human involvement, had not been bruised by such a quiet and understanding rejection. All his capacity for a selfless and unembarrassed devotion found its centre, burst forth and flowered. He allowed himself to experience the joy of protection rather than possession, of understanding heightened and perfectly balanced by a denial of physical intimacy. During the long evenings which they spent together and in others that followed, they achieved a communion of spirit which at times bordered on intoxication. What neither of them realized was that they were indulging something which demands a complete equality of temperament, and is possible only for two men of very masculine natures. Eddie with his streak of indolent sensuality could not keep it up, especially as the months passed and the shock of Maurice's death became a little less painful.

Aware of the other's powerful masculinity, yielding to it as was his nature, and denied by his own will of that consummation which was as natural to him as a certain degree of asceticism was to Jim, Eddie made the first fatal move. Inevitably, his sensibility heightened by constant association with the type of companion which in other circumstances he would long since have yielded to, he sought his pleasure elsewhere – and found it. At first these encounters had been fleeting, but in time they became more and more necessary, until the facade began to crumble and he became furtive. Long before the night when Abraham Gillespie turned up on the doorstep, maudlin and drunk, Jim sensed what was going on and was sick at heart. A spell had been broken, and neither of them knew what the next move would be.

III

'The La is cooking supper. I'll just have time to have a bath before I let her in.' Eddie stood up.

'I hope it's not going to be one of her formal inspirations because I'm not going to wear anything heavier than a T-shirt. Not in this weather.'

'You'll have to put on something more formal for Grace's dinner party on Tuesday.' Eddie crossed to the door.

'God, yes. I suppose we'll have to go.' Jim stretched his arms lazily and allowed his heavy shoulders to droop.

Eddie smiled.

'You'll have an opportunity to get to know Paddy a little better. He's coming. Otherwise it's just the three of us here.'

'Does it have a purpose?'

'None that I know of. Just a routine dinner party.'

'Does she know about Bellington and this girl?'

'Not officially, of course,' he replied. 'And I'm quite certain she knows nothing about the drugs. If she did she'd be horrified. But Desmond knows about the book and wants to encourage any help given. So in that way I suppose the party has a purpose.'

'I see.' Jim leaned an elbow on the mantelpiece and allowed his body to sag. 'I'm sorry for that girl.'

'Kate? The drug thing is awful, of course. But otherwise she thinks she's having a big love affair. What she doesn't know is that Paddy tells Desmond all about it and Desmond tells me. Interesting in its way, and very modern.' Eddie gave this piece of gossip dead-pan. Jim turned down his mouth with an expression of distaste.

'How did you find out about her being on hard drugs? Surely Desmond doesn't know that.' Jim's body was no longer limp. He was leaning forward, obviously expecting an answer to something which puzzled him. When Eddie had first mentioned it he had taken the information for granted. Now he wanted to know.

Eddie noticed the change in the atmosphere. When Jim

was uncertain of himself he became aggressive, asserting himself obliquely on matters which did not involve either of them directly. This was a typical case. It was also an embarrassing one for Eddie. He had heard about Kate a few weeks ago in a bar where he was drinking with Abe and a few others. The girl came in accompanied by a benign, white-haired old man who looked like Cardinal Hume. 'That,' said one of the company, 'is one of the biggest drug peddlers in Dublin and the bird is his newest pusher. They work hard for a dose of their own medicine and he gives them enough dough to pay rent and buy food as well. Some of them last as long as two years.' It was a chilling moment and Eddie had no intention of telling Jim about it.

'Of course he doesn't,' he said glibly. 'It's just that one day in the hall a syringe fell out of her bag while she was hurrying out. She's always running. I was coming up from The La and saw her pick it up. Fortunately she didn't see me.'

Jim looked at him hard for a few moments and then shook his head,

'Poor girl,' he murmured with a sigh, 'poor girl.'

Eddie, who had faced the searching stare without flinching, turned away with a sense of relief not altogether unmixed with a certain regret. This was something he would never have got away with with Maurice.

A quarter of an hour later he was drying himself in front of the mirror in the bathroom. He had never been one for a long soak: a vigorous scrub, a quick immersion and he was done. Nor had he ever spent much time in front of looking glasses. But now with the towel hanging loosely about his shoulders he patted his stomach and inspected his own reflected image.

In his youth he had been slight, flaxen-haired and baby-faced. His hair was now darker and thinner and the features which stared back at him were those of a chunky, broad-shouldered, deep-chested man with a slight paunch, whose only mark of effeminacy was the extreme fineness of

176

his skin. He had always walked with rather a heavy tread, and if he shrugged and used his hands a little more expressively than is usual with Irishmen, he knew that this did not really signify anything. He drew his brows together and thrust out his lower lip as he turned away from the mirror.

He forgot about his appearance as he dusted himself with talc and began to dress. As he put on a clean shirt, Eddie reflected on his own good health. Perhaps this was simply due to the fact that he had never attempted to thwart his own nature, had accepted himself for what he was from a very early age. But what about Maurice? Had he never come to terms with himself? Or had the damage been done before they met? He sprinkled some cologne on his handkerchief and tried to forget about the whole thing.

But it kept moving about like a night creature in the back of his mind all during supper, and made the encounter which he knew would take place later in the evening even more frenetic. His mind rejected what was going to take place while his body, warm, scented, well-fed and healthy grew more and more restless with damped-down excitement. He knew he would have welcomed a quiet night, mooning about, listening to records, going to bed early, and allowing his thoughts to expand, explore, rearrange: it was precisely the sort of night he was not going to have: and perversely he did not want to change it.

Supper was routine. Recently the three of them had fallen into the habit of eating together in Eddie's flat. It dated from the early days after Maurice's death and was already becoming a bit of a strain, but none of them knew how to break it up without giving offence.

'Que bella insalata,' murmured The La eyeing the empty bowl as they lingered over the coffee. A moment before Eddie had caught her glancing at her wrist watch. Half-eight.

'Well of course,' he replied brightly. 'No one can make salad like you.'

'And no one buys as much of it as you. Impossible not to make something good out of all that lettuce and vegetables.'

177

'I didn't make the salad dressing. You can spoil that even with the best eggs and oil.'

'You can spoil anything,' said Jim unexpectedly. The La flashed him an inquiring glance while Eddie stared into his cup. But Jim avoided her eyes.

Later in the sitting room, as they waited for The La to finish washing up and join them, he was back in line, a little too contrite and eager for comfort, but generally much as he always was on evenings such as this.

'Politics,' said The La coming in and taking over. 'I won't have that. Let's talk about something human. Did I tell you I met that woman who's minding Dolly Hughes for the Alcoholics. I didn't? Well, I persuaded Dolly to bring her in, expecting the worst, and do you know, the woman is a saint. Works all day in the civil service and spends her nights driving round looking after people like Dolly.'

'When was this?' said Eddie politely. This was obviously a topic which The La had been saving up for a sticky evening.

'Oh, one day last week. Dolly hasn't had a single slip – that's what they call it, it meant something else in my day – since she gave up the bottle. She's a Mrs Winters, a widow with no children. I think little Dolly is completely cured but she was quite vexed with me when I told her so. Says you never are and that you only live from day to day – and then only by relying on other people as well as trying to help them. It's like a new religion.'

'No,' said Jim quietly, 'only the old one put to some good use.'

'There's a marvellous new singer in America,' went on The La quickly. 'Pills, Spills, some barbaric name like that. My little attache was raving about her the other night. A coloratura. You must get one of her records, Eddie, so that I can hear her. What passes for singing nowadays, e troppo.'

At half-nine Jim said he would go out for a walk and Eddie felt a spasm of anxiety at the prospect of being left alone with The La. She looked at him searchingly for a moment and he smiled at her blandly. But they went on

178

talking about singers. At ten she looked at the clock and stood up.

'Bath night,' she announced. 'I'm going to wallow, what are you going to do?'

'Read a book and go to bed early.'

She touched his hair lightly with her fingers, a motherly pat.

'Yes,' she said gravely, 'you do that.'

IV

Eddie was fully aware that there was something ominous in such perfect tact. The La in particular had not made one false move, while the few discordant notes which Jim struck were quickly covered up. It was rather like a song and dance act in which the singer was a great deal more accomplished than the dancer. When people behaved in a manner so smoothly accommodating it usually indicated that there was little chance of acceptance and none at all of a showdown.

For the moment Eddie was grateful. It was now more than two months since he had begun to entertain Abraham Gillespie on Saturday nights. Nothing was said after the first disastrous occasion, when the big docker hammered on the door drunk and maudlin after Eddie left him in a bar and came home. The La and Jim heard the altercation in the hall during which Eddie succeeded in pacifying the noisy visitor, sending him home in a contrite mood. When the following Saturday Eddie mentioned at supper that he was expecting a caller the others behaved with instinctive grace. Since then the comedy had been polished to a high gloss. No one was under any illusion as to how much the other knew. They all knew.

Now, as he moved about his room restlessly, Eddie was aware of something fluid and uncontained in its atmosphere. Objects reflecting the light, the surfaces of tables, ornaments and the treacherous depths of mirrors shimmered and glowed, and appeared at brief moments to be on the point of dissolving, before a step on the part of the occupant restored them to their familiar shape. The curtains were drawn, but outside Eddie knew that it was still quite bright with the soft deceiving haze of long summer evenings. The clock on the mantelpiece whirred and struck half-ten, cutting through the silence like a butter knife tapping a plate after slicing off a segment. And five minutes afterwards the bell rang.

The man who came into the room had changed a great

180

deal since Eddie first met him in the Rainbow Inn. Changed even more since he had turned up uninvited at the front door, and found himself staring at a couple of strange faces who appeared behind Eddie in the hall. The episode remained a vague blurr which crystallized into a sharp sense of guilt. Eddie said very little about it when they next met. If he had it would have meant the end of that particular association, a conclusion which both of them expected for very different reasons. Eddie was prepared for defiance, sullen accusation, even violence. Abraham, anticipating a sharp malicious rebuke of the sort to which he was all too accustomed, felt his guilt recoil upon him before the older man's unexpressed sadness at what had taken place. He did not try to justify himself, would not in fact have known how to do so in the face of such gentleness, which covered, he knew not how, a terrible fatalistic grief.

The old attitudes acquired in the course of a hundred one-night stands seemed altogether inappropriate now. They chatted uneasily in the garish atmosphere of the Rainbow and, almost at the same moment, both of them felt the necessity of leaving it. They went to another quieter place and there, bereft of a backdrop carefully calculated to encourage hysteria, Abraham managed to stammer out a few words of apology. Eddie immediately realized that the change of scene was largely accountable for this sudden deepening of their tenuous relationship. But the fact that it happened at all indicated on his part the acceptance of a responsibility. Another person had made a fumbling effort to be understood and had not been repulsed. For the first time in his life Abraham Gillespie, crashing about in a jungle where an ape-like bellow had hitherto been his sole means of silencing the shrill jabbering about him, found himself at the edge of a still pool gazing at his own image and not liking what he saw.

At the end of that evening Eddie knew that he had committed himself to the education of something untamed and confused. But this time the mystery was entirely on the other side. Eddie found himself under the necessity of being polite and thoughtful. So far the rewards on a certain level

181

were as much as many people achieved in a whole lifetime. There was something, he told himself wryly, to be said for the tactile.

'You're looking very spruce tonight,' he said approvingly, carefully trying to hide his satisfaction by holding his head on one side and pulling down the corners of his mouth. 'What have you been doing?'

'I was at home, painting the kitchen.' Abraham smiled ruefully and looked down at his hands as if he expected to find some spots of paint on them. When he looked up Eddie's expression had changed. He was smiling a question.

'Me mother thinks I've got religion.'

'Perhaps you have.'

'I've got a thirst.'

Eddie went to the cabinet and poured out a large whiskey and soda. He left it down on the table in front of the sofa.

'Take off your coat, Abie. It's warm.'

Abraham patted his breast pocket with its neatly folded white handkerchief and squared his massive shoulders. In one respect he had not changed. His well-made light-weight blue suit, which was almost devoid of padding, was a present from Eddie, as was his white shirt, red silk tie and suede shoes. As he took off his jacket and folded it carefully over a chair before taking up his drink, Eddie realized the full significance of his new circle's ill-concealed jealousy. Abraham was a beautifully built male animal, with the face of a slightly tarnished pagan idol. But the tarnish no longer represented an over-indulgence in beer. The flabbiness of cheek and paunch had disappeared in the last few months during which he had cut down drastically on his drinking. He was pathetically trying to live up to his new clothes, unaware that he was paying for them with something rarer than cash.

'You're not having anything?'' he enquired as he sniffed his drink.

'Not at the moment.' Eddie sat down in the armchair and shook his head. An evening at home painting the kitchen was not to be taken as an excuse for a celebration. There were other methods of intoxication which Abraham was only just discovering. 'I'm taking a good look at you.'

'What?' The big man, who was about to lower himself onto the sofa, straightened up, his stomach rigid, his chin thrust forward. He seemed uncertain of whether he was being admired or appraised.

'The house painting is doing you good. You look about ten years younger than you did six months ago.'

Abraham relaxed and a slow smile of innocent pleasure spread over his broad face.

'If I go on like this, I might be able to take up boxing again. I won a belt when I was eighteen.'

'I didn't know that. Is that why some people think you're dangerous? I was told you were.'

'If you listen to some people they'll tell you plenty about me. I knocked out a couple of them the first few months I started to go to the Rainbow. Some people think they can treat you like dirt.' He sat down and stared into his glass. 'They weren't like you,' he went on in a low voice, almost as if he were talking to himself. Then he looked up slowly and smiled.

Eddie felt a curious sense of defeat; that coiling sensation of suffocation sometimes experienced by those who have achieved their objective only too well. He knew what that smile meant, knew also that he had deliberately provoked it. The strange feeling of fluidity, of something mysterious and still unrealized at the back of his mind, swept over him again for a moment, as if to heighten the intensity of the reaction which it always produced. His mind was not yet prepared for it, but his body in its own wisdom knew that some day that strange stirring of the imagination would be transfixed, analysed, catalogued and set in order, and for the moment it rebelled, lending him a seductiveness beyond his intentions, so that every action, glance and word were filled with that phosphorescent grace which has little to do with the definition of sex, and nothing at all with good looks. If he had been a womaniser, his victims would have felt its straining potency as strongly as Abraham felt it now. Eddie was a man on the point of feeding upon his own chaos and

183

for the moment that dionysiac element ran riot. If he had denied himself his pleasure now he would indeed have invited sickness.

He reached forward suddenly, took the glass from Abraham's hand, drank half of it, stood up and held it to the other man's lips. He felt his hands covered as the glass was drained. It fell on the carpet between them as his wrists were grasped and he allowed himself to be mercifully drawn down and held with strangely gentle fingers as he fed upon the potency which in its turn was offered to him.

'That isn't enough,' whispered Abraham later, lifting the hot dishevelled body by the armpits and stroking the naked chest with his palms. Eddie shivered and looked up with gratitude into eyes as glazed as his own. Slowly like two people shocked by an accident they made their way into the hall and through the kitchen into the bedroom.

Afterwards, sated and filled with that urgency which passive natures experience after the pain and pleasure of their submission, Eddie sat up in the bed, grasped his hands about his knees and stared at the moonlight streaming through the window. Abraham, thinking he was weeping, touched his shoulder gently.

'This is when the others always wanted me to go out. That was how I knew you were different.'

'I wonder if I am.' Eddie realized that he wished to God Abraham would go home, and felt a little ashamed at the thought.

'Not in some ways. That's the same.' Abraham spoke slowly, as if he were repeating a lesson he had taught himself. It was never easy for him to express himself, but Eddie noticed more than once that he dropped a remark which revealed that he was not as dumb as he pretended to be. He had his full share of native cunning.

'When it comes to the bit and you want it, I'm just a big cock, and you like it that way, and so do I. But would you like it if I told you that you're just a nice piece of ass? Or that you blow me real good the way I like it?'

'Poetic justice.' Eddie was suddenly sobered; quiet, a little tense. 'I think I'd take it as a compliment.'

'Yaw.' There was an edge in Abraham's voice, not menacing, but defiant. 'You could take it that way OK and I might even believe you. But that's because you have other things going for you. All them books and records and nobs of friends. Suppose I told you I'd like to move in here and never go home again? You think I like labouring on the fucking docks? It was you that told me I'd be different if I moved out of the Rainbow and got myself into some sort of trim again. Maybe you're just cuter than the others. I fuck better this way. But leastways you took some trouble about it. That's what I mean about you being different. You talked to me like I was human or something. You told me I'd never be anything but a slob hanging around the Rainbow. Well, I'm outa that now, and even if I'm staying at home more often and painting the fucking kitchen that doesn't say I like it any better there. And you got friends here. They wouldn't put out the welcome mat for me, even if I fitted in here. So maybe you'd better tell me what I'm supposed to be.'

Eddie knew that Abraham possessed the gigolo temperament in full measure: passive in all things, except the service he was expected to perform. Hitherto he had been content to pay for that. But he wondered now if he was wise in taking this man from the background in which he had found him, in circumstances that exaggerated the gulf between them. The layabout with his limited repertoire of heavy-handed touches had turned out to be a little more complicated than he had bargained for: a gigolo who wanted to invent an identity for himself. Eddie thought that he understood some of his dilemma.

During the past few months he had been introduced into a world where good manners, even when automatic, helped to smooth out the rough edges of life; where subjects were discussed which Abraham did not always understand but felt teased and flattered by their introduction; where music was played and his own passion for Viennese waltzes indulged and encouraged; where he was not paid for his services in hard

185

cash and shown the door, but was instead dressed and presented in respectable public view like the gentlemen he so grudgingly admired. And now he found himself more disorientated than ever. The distance between the little house in Ballyfermot and the grim puritan background which had nurtured, as it so often does, a pagan soul, was far greater from Eddie's world than the conventional clowning in the Rainbow, or the anonymous encounters in hotel rooms.

'Oh, Abie, I could analyze both us out of existence, and where would it get us? Back to where we are.' Eddie turned and looked at the other's face in the softened shadows that sloped over the bed from the beam of moonlight.

'To this.' Abraham caught his hand and pressed it against the damp hair on his naked chest, and then attempted to force it down to the centre of his loins. But Eddie snatched it away and touched his lover's shoulder instead.

'No, not always,' Eddie said gently. 'You know that.'

He felt himself drawn down, his head pressed the hard matted chest. It seemed to him that Abraham's breathing was irregular and congested. He reached up and touched the man's face. It was dry. 'You don't have to pity me,' Abraham muttered. 'I'm no moaner. It's just that I wish I was a complete eejit instead of only a half one.'

And suddenly their whole relationship fell into place. Eddie felt stricken with remorse. How much of his attitude had been one of condescension? How could the other have divined that apart from his sexual prowess he was an object of pity – taken care of, humoured like a child; used.

'There are those who pity *me*,' he murmured in self-defence. It was not a word he should have repeated, but the unexpected accusation and its revelation of a mind aware of its own fumbling ineptitude took him off guard. As if in compensation for this reversal of roles he felt a violent upsurge of desire.

'Yaw, yaw, mebbe. But you don't have to pity me. I earn good money, and I cut down on the booze, didn't I?'

Eddie drew away and lay on his back staring at the

186

flickering brook of moonlight. This was how it was to be, a length of cock and little else; exactly the same as being a nice piece of ass. Strange tides moved and coiled within him; knowledge dimly glimpsed and secreted in an obscure corner of his mind. Another layer removed from the swaddled infant of human innocence. An experience out of which someday a clear precise arrangement of events would somehow emerge.

But it was too late for analysis now.

V

The hawthorns were dying in a flush of hectic pink and all the scents of summer came floating in the open window; stock and lilac were cut through with the sharp fresh tang of newly-mown grass. The beeches threw indolent shadows over the yellow-green lawn, a little too closely cut that afternoon, and the men walked back and forwards on the gravel paths, in and out of the sunlight as if they were pacing a long gallery lit by high arched windows. Eddie and Patrick on one path, Desmond and Jim on the other. Occasionally they called across to one another, and the sound of their voices, thrown back by the blood-red walls, hot and brittle after a long day's sun, came through the window with a curious reverberant echo; the window at which Grace and Maria were sitting at either side in after-dinner ease, watching the men. They were calm, comfortable and a little sleepy, but there was a guarded disquiet in their eyes and The La sighed as she sipped her glass of Kummel.

'Eddie is running wild,' she said as she watched him strolling, looking at the ground, while Patrick, his slim frame stiffened by self-interest, explained something to him with a brisk prodding forefinger.

'I know.' Grace shifted in her chair and narrowed her eyes. 'Is it very bad?'

'Not in itself, I suppose, but in the circumstances . . .' The La shrugged, a gesture which did not suggest an easy mediterranean acceptance, but something careful and anxious.

'Jim?' Grace looked at him. He was listening to Desmond with a polite smile which concealed everything but boredom.

'He knows, of course, all a fine del trimestre. Those two know each other too well. It is very difficult for both of them.' The La looked up at the castle, its small windows yellow-eyed in the blaze of the western sun.

'And says nothing. Jim, I mean.'

'None of us say anything. Che vuole?'

'I don't suppose things can go on like that indefinitely.'

'Of course not.' The La waved an impatient hand. At that moment, Eddie looked up and, taking it for a greeting, raised his hand in reply. Maria, actress swift, softened her gesture and smiled.

'He has charm, that one,' she murmured. 'He draws people to him.' She turned to Grace with a very different expression, hard and wise.

'It could go on if they were different people. But that's the whole point. They will come to terms with their own lives in their own way. Our little Eddie is quite capable of coping. This is a phase, it was bound to happen. But I worry about the other one. He is not made to stand still. Soon he will have to do something. The retreat is over. What is he going to do, cara? You know him better than I.'

'I doubt it.' Grace smiled at the golden head bent over its glass of liqueur. 'I've been talking to the bishop. He's read Jim's book, a proof copy.'

'Ah.' The La breathed a low sigh and looked at Jim as he turned aside to say something to Desmond. 'I thought it would come to that. He has nothing more to say, nothing more to write. He has worked it out of his system.'

'The bishop didn't say that.' Grace frowned gravely.

'Of course he didn't.' The La gave a cynical, thoroughly Italian smile. 'Perhaps if you tell me what he did say I might be able to interpret.'

Grace paused a moment, then relaxed and the two women exchanged a smile. The world of men, it seemed to say, oh no.

'It's the sort of book Dr Curley says he might have written himself if he was younger and able to express himself as well as Jim.' There was a note of pride in her voice. 'It gives a very objective description of the state of the Church in Europe, movements, new thoughts, priestly attitudes and so on ...'

'And ends up by saying that it's just another crisis that Roma is passing through, that the truth will emerge from all the talk, all the silly books, and that the rock will stand. All its mistakes, all its stupidity will not prevail against it,

I know, I know. Is that it?'

'Yes, more or less, that's it.' Grace chuckled. 'I think you *do* know him better than I.'

'And now?' The La raised an eyebrow and lifted her long rope of artificial pearls on one finger; a slender chain of milky pink in the shimmer of contrasting light.

'We must wait, I suppose.'

'Yes.' The La narrowed her eyes and looked at Eddie's back. He turned and was walking towards the end of the garden on the dappled grass. Patrick and he stepped off the gravel.

'It is strange. Perhaps there *is* something in the fall of a sparrow. Which is why we shall never know ourselves. If we did, then indeed there would be no hope for us, and little mercy. As it is we work out our own destiny in the dark. What moves us to do so? Even Eddie's little madness is not without its meaning. Who knows? If anybody does he will himself, perhaps soon, perhaps a long time from now. He has that sort of gift. It will save him from much evil. But at the moment he is simply acting according to his nature. I think we are all right to keep silent.' She sipped her Kummel, and Grace fell in with her mood. They both realized that any further discussion of this particular topic would border on gossip, speculation, prurient curiosity.

A perfect summer evening: a pause, a gathering of forces, trees and flowers keeping their mystery as closely as the furniture and objects in the room behind them reflected the light in a burnished glow. Mute spectators, outliving human aspirations; a silent reproach to folly. How much of it had those old trees and walls, those cherished pieces of furniture witnessed in their time? The La finished her Kummel and looked about her. She had a strange feeling of being watched and sensed that the moment had come for a lighter topic.

'What do you think of our lordling?' she said with a little silvery laugh.

'Paddy?' Grace's voice was eager. She too was anxious to get on to lighter matters.

'Patrick. Paddy. Lord Bellington. Whatever you like to

call him. I suppose he's pumping Eddie about his book. He's been helping him to correct it, you know.'

'So Desmond tells me. I believe it's going to be very naughty. All Palmerston's love affairs. I'm told he used to wander about Windsor at night turning all the door-handles.' Grace made a face of mock disgust, and laughed.

'Just the sort of thing that would appeal to Bellington.' There was real dislike in The La's voice and Grace looked at her sharply. But her friend was looking out the window. In the garden the quartet changed sides. Desmond walked over to Eddie and Patrick joined Jim. 'And now he's pumping Jim, I suppose.'

'Oh, he's harmless.'

'I wonder.'

'You don't like him?'

'No.' The La's voice held a note of finality. She was thinking of Maurice and of how much she missed him. Grace, who felt the same, said nothing. And after all what harm could an ambitious, promiscuous young man with literary pretensions do to anyone? She knew nothing of Kate's real role, and The La thought it wiser not to tell her, a decision she was afterwards to regret. At the moment Paddy provided an excuse for shifting the conversation to a less strained topic.

'Oh well,' said Grace, leaning forward and looking out. At that moment Eddie glanced up at the window and the two women stared back at him. They had their own thoughts and he experienced a curious sensation, a little like the one we feel in a strange place; I have been here before. The tangled threads of intimacy and emotions that bound the four men together in the outdoor drawing room that the garden had become that evening. The two women watching. A chorus. I shall remember this, he thought, as they drifted back towards the house, feeling the chill as the wall turned to bronze and the shadows gathered in their inscrutable secrets, as men carry the burden of knowledge they do not always understand.

191

VI

'Phew, this heat is killing me.'

The bishop blew out his cheeks and mopped his forehead with a large old fashioned check handkerchief. It was faded and Jim smiled as he looked at it. Nuns used to use them in the old days and the bishop must have had it a very long time.

'You might as well get accustomed to it. It's good training.' Standing at the open window Jim looked down at the dusty square, with the trunks of the trees behind the railing whitened by passing traffic.

'That's supposed to be finished. But one has to get used to the climate by experience. However they tell me it's very good on account of the height of the place. Sao Paulo is well up over the coast and they have snow in winter, which is now.'

'When are you off?'

'Sometime in August. In time for the spring out there.' Dr Curley tucked his handkerchief into the cuff of his light summer jacket. 'Have you sent off your proofs?'

Jim turned and looked at the neat brown parcel on his desk. It had been lying there for two days, ready for posting. When it was gone there would be a void.

'Not yet. I intended to send it off today.'

'Good. I enjoyed it.'

'More than I have, perhaps. There doesn't seem much else to say.'

'Plenty to do, Jim.'

The two men looked at each other for a moment, both knowing exactly what the other was thinking. Then Jim came back from the window and poured out some more orangeade for his visitor. His own glass was almost untasted. He settled down in a chair facing the empty fireplace, his back to the desk.

'How did Jack Wilson's consecration go off?'

'The same as mine with a few trimmings cut out. I felt queer, like a ghost. And in a way I was, because in the old

192

days I'd have been dead. A strange feeling.'

'Yes, it must have been.' Jim thought of his own reactions at Maurice's High Mass. He looked down at his shoes and made a decision. The devil, a stirring of obscure psychological motives, a simple hatred of the institutional church; different people would have given him different answers for what he had experienced. Why not sound out this old man with whom in a way his long pilgrimage had begun? 'What would you have felt if the whole thing had struck you as obscene?'

'Obscene?' The bishop opened his eyes wide, then pursed his lips. 'A little unreal, certainly. I felt I didn't belong, redundant. After all, you have written that ritual expresses a need. Perhaps there is too much of it, and it appears meaningless to many now. But somewhere, hidden behind it there is something that we all want to know. Or deliberately reject.'

'Did you feel apathetic?'

'I'm afraid I did, a little.' Curley spoke, frowning, stroking his sagging jowls thoughtfully. 'The worst of all, I suppose. But it may have been that my life in that particular place was ended and I was really thinking of other things.' He looked at Jim sharply. 'Did you feel apathetic at that High Mass?'

Jim shifted his position, crossing his legs and balancing his glass on his knee. For a moment the bottom of the glass was cool and pleasurable on his skin through the thin material of his trousers. Then it began to take heat from his body. Grace would have told the old man about the funeral. An ambulance went wailing by outside and as it died away something fell on the floor above. He knew Kate was with Patrick.

'No. Just violent. I wanted to get away from it all. Since I couldn't, the body took over. Images, fancies, things I never knew I could imagine.' He looked at Curley with a hard, defiant stare, but the bishop seemed no more than deeply attentive.

'There are few things we cannot imagine,' he said simply. 'Especially when our emotions are confused. It must have

193

been that sort of an occasion for you.' He ran his fingers along the rim of his collar.

'I should have thought you would be able to work out that aspect of it yourself.'

Thus, Jim thought, was Eddie dismissed and the ghost of Maurice. And of course it was a personal problem, the details of which he had no intention of telling his visitor. This time he could not accuse him of blandness.

'In my day,' he heard him go on, 'we would have called that sort of thing simply temptation. Perhaps they have some other word for it now. But it still remains temptation. Ultimately it's a choice. You either accept or reject. It's usually for personal reasons and if these seem valid to you, nothing that you do is a rejection. You may leave the Church, but if you take on another responsibility, a human one perhaps, then you must accept that the old church, muddled and fusty though it may seem, means a great deal to other people. So in a way if we act out of charity we never really reject. But sometimes, somewhere, we've got to make up our minds how we are going to act, and for what reason, and for whom.' He slumped back in his chair and sighed noisily, expelling air jerkily through his mouth as his broad shoulders bumped against the chair. 'If I may say so, Jim, I think that your problem is that you don't really know what you want.'

This so neatly described Jim's state of mind for some time past that he was irritated.

'You think I'm incapable of decision?' he said coldly.

'All this.' The bishop waved his hand, as if he wanted to include the whole way of life which Jim had made for himself. 'It's very pleasant, I'm sure, and you deserve it. After all you made it yourself, without any help from me. But unless I'm mistaken, you don't really have that kind of temperament. If you wrote out of your imagination, yes, this is ideal, but you don't. You've analyzed everything, or at least the things you're interested in.' He leaned forward and tapped the arm of his chair. 'Have you come up with any real final answers, anymore than the rest of us? Are you sure any longer even of the questions? All this thinking and analyzing is no good, unless you do something. Get yourself involved with people. Put all those theories that you have into action. After this last book there doesn't seem to be anything else to do.'

Jim got up and walked the length of the room. It reminded him of something, someplace he could not quite recall. The carpet with its snuff-coloured base and its worn pattern of subtle grey-green and blue colours; the sun pouring into the windows and the shadows thrown by the walls between; the tops of the trees across the road outside; the delicate scent of sweet pea from the bowl on his desk. It was like Grace's garden the other evening after dinner.

He wondered just exactly what he was. A priest who could not attend a church service without a feeling of nausea. Could that have been simply an outburst of sexual jealousy, an outburst of hidden, well-controlled appetite? The bishop had called it emotional confusion. He might just be right; and it had happened at a time of great strain. It was one of the most vivid experiences of his life, yet when he sat down to write about the institution of which that little country church was a tiny part (and its ministers not even representative) he found that in cold blood he could not condemn it. He was gnawing at the kernel and it would not break. He could not gnaw for ever. It was time to act – that he felt in his bones.

He turned, resting his knuckles on the desk and asked the question which had hovered between them since the bishop's first visit.

'You want me to go with you, don't you?'

'Yes, I do.' The old man's answer was prompt and effective. If he had temporized now, Jim would have matched his sophistry with a very polite rejection. But the proposal was laid on the line bluntly and without trimmings. At least one of them knew how to act; and the other responded.

"A priest who does not believe in half of the dogmas of the church, who cannot enter a church without wanting to throw up?' There was an undercurrent of excitement in Jim's voice. The quiet days were over, and he suddenly realized how much they had been thrust upon him by circumstances. He had adapted himself well but it was a long time since he felt so keenly and aggressively alive.

'A priest who believes in God when he might very well have confused him with the institution, who still thinks charity is the only answer, that it is better to love than be loved.' Jim started at this last statement, but the bishop did not seem to notice it. 'And who has the power of absolution.' He took out his check handkerchief again and wiped the perspiration from his nose.

'A man who has no answers. Aren't we supposed to have some at least?' He was no longer leaning on the desk, but standing upright, bending a little forward, his eyes fixed on the faded square of check cotton.

'Answers can freeze a man, dry up his humanity. I discovered that, late in the day, perhaps. But at least I discovered it.' Suddenly Curley looked up with a shrewd narrowing of the eyes. 'I think you'll do, if you'll only relax, stop thinking too much about yourself. Get involved with other people, see how they act on you instead of trying to influence them. And forget that you were ever meant to be a judge. There are lots of people who want help, not answers, just help. You don't have to be in the pulpit to give that. There are lots of things you can do. You needn't even minister if you don't want to. But I think when you see some of the people out there you might be glad that you have the power of forgiving. At no time, unless I'm much mistaken, have you ever denied that. Or do you want to do so now?'

Jim had a feeling that he had been waiting a very long time for this moment and that what he was being offered was the final temptation; the age-old seduction of Rome. The rock; the keeper of the keys; the guardian of the word. The wisdom of the serpent, an abiding mystery, encrusted with the fading gems of centuries of pathetic human tribute; sublime even in its folly, concealing a few very simple truths under a mountain, man-made and landscaped with a thousand superficial images and a wilderness of aromatic herbs. Was there a smile concealed

196

behind this tremendous human assumption? A sovereign bedecked in Byzantine robes, waiting with inscrutable weariness for a child to smile with him in private at all the pretensions of the audience chamber. A trap, not for the unwary, but for the wise.

He was about to reply when they were interrupted by a knock on the door. Jim raised his eyebrows in surprise and went to open it. Kate Vale stood outside holding a cardboard file in her hands. She smiled into Jim's blank face.

'Patrick asked me to leave this here for Mr Doyle.' Without any further explanation she came into the room, saw the bishop and stopped dead, holding the file against her breast. 'Oh, I'm terribly sorry, I didn't know you had a visitor.' The bishop nodded benignly and smiled. 'Is Mr Doyle here?'

'I think he's out.'

'But ...' Kate bit her lip and looked about. 'Isn't this his flat?'

'He lives downstairs, on the ground floor.' Jim looked at her sharply. The pupils of her eyes were slightly enlarged, but she seemed quite in control of herself.

'Oh, my God. Patrick said just downstairs. This is part of the manuscript. You know how Mr Doyle reads it for him. But if he's out ...' Her eyes wandered to the bookcase. 'Oh, Mr Dillingham, *The Sacred Fount*, I've been looking for it for years.' She crossed quickly to the bookcase and took out the dark-red scrolled volume – the 1901 first edition – and began to flick through it with her back to them. The two men looked at each other and waited politely. When Jim turned back she was replacing the book with one hand. The file in her other hand was open.

'I suppose I daren't ask you for the loan of it?' Her voice was breathless, excited.

'Well ...'

'I know, I know. People are so horrible about returning books. But you might relent sometime.' She looked down at the open file and closed it. 'What shall I do with this?'

'You can leave it here if you like or slip it under his door. It's usually locked.' Jim had a curious feeling that she knew

197

all this perfectly well already and could not have mistaken the flat so easily. But perhaps she was a little confused. And she seemed to be fumbling both with the book and the cardboard file. An odd incongruous intrusion.

'Yes, I think I'd better do that. How very stupid of me. I think it must be all this typing, it makes me a little dizzy sometimes. Do forgive me.' She seemed relieved about something and flashed a genuinely warm smile at Jim and his guest, then disappeared as suddenly as she had come, bringing the file with her.

'The visitor from Porlock,' said the bishop, getting up with a wry smile. 'Perhaps it's just as well. It'll give you time to think things over. You will do that, won't you?'

'Yes, I will. I think you probably know the answer already.'

'In that case I'll call again soon. A week perhaps?'

'Yes, of course. I may not have decided finally by then, but come anyhow.'

The old man patted him gently on the arm as they went out. Jim went back upstairs and looked at his watch. Five o'clock. He walked up and down the room with long purposeful strides, stopping only to go to the window to get a breath of air. He reached his hand out and felt the brick beside the sash; it was warm and dry from the long sunny days and it gave him a strange sense of security. A century and a half of exposure, and it still responded to the sun. Perhaps if men felt as little they would live as long.

At six he heard Eddie coming in and went down to enquire about the manuscript. It had not been slipped under the door but a few days earlier she had come in looking for Patrick, and pounced upon another volume of Henry James – *The Reverberator* – in Eddie's bookcase. He had not loaned it to her either.

'Perhaps she really is a James fan,' said Jim doubtfully.

'No, just doped to the eyes. She knows perfectly well which flat is which. Have a drink Jim, you look as if you'd seen a ghost.'

'I still can't make it out.'

'Oh, balls,' said Eddie cheerfully. 'Just think, no Palmerston tonight. What'll you have?'

VII

The black Vauxhall drew up in front of Greg as he was walking up Barnhill Road on his way home after buying an evening paper in Dalkey. It was his day off and he was wearing sloppy grey flannels and a white shirt. The young man who hopped out of the car presented a very different appearance; tight orange slacks, mauve shirt-jacket, rolled sleeves, a silver bracelet on one wrist, elaborately wide watch band on the other. His thick fair hair, bleached by the sun, was worn long, and he raked it back with his fingers as a gust of wind whirled around the corner. He raised his thumb in greeting, and Greg who had been studying the number of the car, nodded back. He recognized the plate and the call-sign. Sierra Twenty. The drugs squad.

'Hullo Dick,' he said. 'What are you up to tonight?'

'The usual. I want to ask you something. We can sit in the car. I've left Joe Coyne in a pub in Dalkey.'

This did not surprise Greg. He knew that members of the squad rarely travelled alone. He knew Coyne – a quiet middle-aged man who was something of a father figure in the drugs scene in Dublin – only slightly, but Dick Grogan was the son of an old friend in the force who came from Greg's part of the country. This lean handsome young man, with the face of a television cowboy hero, had a curious reputation often discussed by the older men in the stations, not always with approval. He was generally supposed to sleep around quite a lot; had been for a time the lover of a wife of a government minister; smoked pot; procured contraceptives for contacts in the game, and delighted in shocking the more conventional members of the force by his unorthodox behaviour. But no one could deny that he got results. As Greg slid into the car beside him he felt a cold sense of foreboding.

'You've got friends in Fitzwilliam Square.' Grogan came to the point at once, leaning his back against the door and searching his colleague's face with his cold grey eyes. Greg shifted uncomfortably and rolled the newspaper on his lap.

'Yes, I know Eddie Doyle. You've probably heard of his family from your father. You don't mean to tell me he's on drugs.'

'No, he's not.' Grogan grinned, a stagey automatic widening of his chiselled mouth. 'And neither is The La, nor the other fellow that lives there, Dillingham, the ex-priest. But there's a new tenant who smokes pot, chap by the name of Lord Bellington.'

'Oh.' Greg waited, recovering his composure. He had heard about Patrick, but he did not see what all this had to do with him now, especially since Eddie was not involved.

'He has a girl friend, the lord I mean. Bird called Vale. English. A bit of a layabout. I used to meet her on the scene.'

Greg began to feel nettled. Why all this drama, and on his day off too?

'I thought you turned a blind eye to marijuana.' There was a touch of sarcasm in his voice. A young girl passed in a very tight skirt, gave a quick sidelong look at Grogan and passed on with a smile. Greg could imagine the success he must have whenever he was in the mood, and felt a sharp stab of envy. The young, the free, the beautiful and heedless hedonists. But Grogan did not seem impressed by this particular girl. No doubt he had his pick.

'So we do. If we didn't we'd never get anything serious done. Besides hash is harmless. There are only seven of us as you know on this particular beat and the smokers know the rules: OK, have your fun, it doesn't do anybody any harm, pass the joint around. But no shit.'

'Yes, so I've heard.' Greg looked down at the headline: a custom-post blown up near Newry. 'You mean the hard stuff.' He felt old and square.

'Cocaine, heroin.' There was a note of patience in Grogan's light husky voice. 'By and large the arrangement works fairly well. It comes in now and again but we have our contacts. They don't really want to get hooked. Joe has shown them a few cases and they know what they're letting themselves in for. They slip us the word. The Vale chick is

200

peddling heroin.' Grogan lit a cigarette with an expensive lighter. A present from the minister's wife?

'Good God!' Greg was automatically appalled as various possibilities loomed. "Is this Bellington fellow on it too?'

'No. We've checked. He's sleeping with her and she passes a few joints around for him. It isn't that. A new operator has moved into Dublin, hoping to make a quick haul before we get on his tail. But he's a diabolical bastard. He knows our methods. No scandal. A working arrangement with the hash scene. Several of our contacts have told us how it's being worked. I expect he's thought it out, but the little Vale cunt is playing along very cutely. She's told several people, all contacts of mine. It was meant to be passed on.'

'Some sort of plant?' Greg did not quite get it yet: this sort of thing was outside his range, just as Dolly's furtive drinking had once been.

'Spot on. That's exactly what it is.' Grogan lowered the window and tapped ash out on the path. Another pretty young girl passed by and smiled at him. When he turned back there was the remains of a grin on his face. But only for an instant. Then the grey eyes hardened, and the voice took on a metallic tone.

'In the ordinary course we'd just run her and the pusher in, plant some snow on them if necessary and put them on the first boat to Liverpool. But do you know what the little hoor has done? She's left small quantities of the stuff here and there in houses that we don't want to raid. You know (he mentioned the name of a famous Irish actor, prominent in the language movement and a friend of the President). Well, she got into his house, pretending to look for a part and dumped a sample there. And there are several others, mostly film people, Trinity professors, business men who play angels in the theatre. We'd have to get warrants to search every one of those houses and it would create one almighty stink. She says they're hookers. We know they're not. Which is where you come in, Greg. She's planted some on your friends in Fitzwilliam Square, the Doyle fellow, Dillingham, even the poor old La.'

201

'Jesus.' Greg was startled into admiration of his old friend's son. No wonder Grogan was allowed to operate in his own way. 'Go on, Dick, I'll do what I can.'

'I thought you might.' The voice was soft now, confidential. 'It's a delaying operation, of course. We still don't know where the real cache is. But even if we lay our hands on it she's going to name every one of these people, and they're all people who mightn't like publicity for various reasons. So we've asked some of our own boys who know them to approach them, explain the position, and agree to a search. I only heard of all this last night, but it's been going on for some time, and every day that passes a few more are hooked and the money in the kitty mounts up.'

'What do you want me to do?'

'I want you to get off your ass and go into Fitzwilliam Square as fast as you can. They'll probably remember that one coming in on some excuse. It should be easy enough to find.'

'Right.' Greg pressed the door handle and then stopped as Grogan laid a hand on his arm.

'There's something else Greg. I know about Doyle. I suppose you do too. It's the sort of thing I hear on the party circuit. What's the odds, so long as he doesn't do it on the street it's OK. I don't go for that particular scene myself, but quite a lot of our contacts are that way. Women too. So what? But Doyle has got himself involved with a fairly dicey character at the moment. Fellow called Gillespie. He's done time.'

'For what?' Greg looked at him with incredulous eyes. He had not felt so frightened and appalled since he found out about Dolly.

'Minors. Boys, girls. Of course he's generally available too and may have changed his tastes. It's been some time now since he was on probation – five or six years. I found out about him when I was checking up on the house. You might tip Doyle off.' He rolled down the window and tossed his cigarette out. It gave Greg time to think and also to change this particular subject.

202

'Did you search the Vale woman's flat?'

'Yes, a break-in job by one of our contacts. If we got a warrant they might blow the gaff before we had time to locate the plants.' He gripped the wheel viciously. 'There was nothing there. Jesus, if I get my hands on that pair I'll screw them gutless and not the way she likes it.'

'What happens even if you locate all the plants?' A horrible possibility began to dawn on Greg. 'Will you be able to get rid of them quietly?'

'Smart, Greg. That's just it. For one thing we may not be able to locate the real cache without taking them in with a warrant. It's likely that her boss will have a cross-channel lawyer – none of the Dublin ones will touch it – and he'll name names. That's what worries me. It was Joe thought of that first. But at least we can clear those we do know about, including your friends. After that we'll just have to get a warrant, and you know that process. The bloody thing has to be signed by a Chief Super before a D.J. Then we'll have to plant some of the stuff in her flat, as well as the old man's, and swoop on her before she has time to get rid of it. OK, it's not orthodox, but you can't fight those bastards with laws made after Magna Carta.'

'I'll go now.' Greg opened the door and turned back giving a set smile. 'Thanks Dick. You're your father's son.' It was clumsy but sincere.

'Fuck off,' said Grogan with a grin. 'If my old man knew some of the things I'm in on, he'd make a pilgrimage to Lough Derg and walk all the way in his bare feet.' He took out an envelope, scribbled on it and gave it to Greg. 'That's a number. I'll be there about midnight. Ring me if you find anything. And Greg, tell your friend Doyle to play it safe. This gang's in a big way. God knows what they'll stir up if they're concerned. OK, get going. And next time you see my old man tell him I'm working nights for the Legion of Mary.'

VIII

It was with a sense of relief that Eddie settled down that evening with a biography of Colette, knowing that the night was his. Jim had gone out for a walk; The La was going to bed early to recharge the batteries for a reception at the Italian Embassy next day; and the biography was pleasant reading. Besides he knew that he would be able to put it down now and again, and allow his mind to play about the story which was forming slowly but inexorably in his mind. The reviews had given him a certain confidence, stirred an ambition long dormant, and led him to hope that he had certain powers which would make the years ahead less barren. He would recreate the past.

When his door bell rang a little after eight he put down his book with a frown of annoyance, and let it ring again before he got up to answer it. When he opened the door and saw Greg's face he knew at once that something was wrong. He felt guilty as he thought of Dolly. He hoped to God she hadn't broken out again. Greg in slacks, with a blue pullover and a white shirt had hardly called just to talk about the weather.

'Is anything wrong?' he said when they were back in the room.

Greg sat down and in his slow professional manner repeated the story he had just heard about Kate Vale. When it was over Eddie went immediately to the bookcase and took down his copy of *The Reverberator*. Inside the title page they found a brown envelope. Greg opened it and found a small quantity of white powder like bread soda in one of the corners.

'Good God,' said Eddie, sitting down and staring at his grim-faced friend.

'Is Mr Dillingham at home?'

'Not at the moment. He's gone out for a walk. Sometimes he goes to a film, but otherwise he's usually back about nine.'

'Then we'll have to wait for him. The La?'

'She said she was going to bed. I suppose I'd better go down and ask her what excuse was made to get into her place.'

Greg blinked and looked away. He was thinking of another occasion when other excuses had been made to get into the old singer's flat. Dolly. Thinking also of the further information which Grogan had given him, and he did not know how he was going to tell Eddie. Heroin was one thing: he was acting as a friend. Personal revelations were a great deal more complicated.

'Listen,' he said as Eddie made for the door, 'try and keep her where she is. I don't want her bursting in here and making a scene.'

Eddie gave him a sharp glance, nodded and went on. In the empty room Greg got up and walked about aimlessly. After all why should he say anything? It was none of his business. Then he thought of Grogan's hint of publication: the house being searched. Tongues wagging. And what exactly was Dillingham's position?

Eddie came back. He handed Greg another brown envelope.

'I got out of that fairly easily. She was in bed, so I asked her if Kate had been in looking for anything recently. Said she thought she'd lost a broach and didn't want to disturb The La in case she might be asleep. It appears our friend called to look at the costumes hung up on the wall. So I went through them and found this in Desdemona's pocket.' He chuckled. 'First time it's been used for that, I bet. Now we'll have to wait for Jim. He told me she was in his room last week, pretending she thought it was mine and took down another Henry James novel to look at. I suppose we'll find another envelope in that. First time the old boy's ever been used for that either. He wouldn't approve.'

Now that they had cleared the house, or nearly, Eddie expected Greg to relax. Instead of which he looked sterner than ever. It was impossible to tell that he was trying to cover an acute embarrassment the only way he knew; his cop-eyed look.

'We might as well have a drink while we're waiting,' said

Eddie, going to the tray. 'I shouldn't be at all surprised if this was one of the nights he went to the pictures. It's just the sort of thing that would happen.' He poured out a stiff whiskey for Greg, hoping that it would help to thaw him out. It was accepted gratefully; the visitor felt that he needed it badly.

'Have you a key to Dillingham's flat?' Greg remained standing, shifting uneasily from one foot to another.

'Of course not, except when he's away.' He chuckled. 'Besides I have enough trouble with my own key, what with locking up to prevent The La from lifting things and the Vale woman from planting them. Which reminds me, what about Paddy Bellington? She's up there a lot. He certainly isn't on heroin, but how do we know she hasn't hidden some in his flat?'

'Can't you tell him too?'

'Not tonight. He's gone home and won't be back for a few days. Besides I'm not sure I'm the one to do it. After all she's his girlfriend, I think you'd better get one of your own men to call, or give him a ring at home.'

'Has she a key to his flat?' Greg looked grimmer than ever. He had just thought of something.

'I don't know. She usually comes in the afternoon when I'm at work. I shouldn't be surprised if she had. Jim would know, he's nearly always here during the day.'

'Supposing that's where the real load is? It would be an ideal place to hide it if she has a key and he's away. As it is they're working on a day to day basis. They may be shifting it around, and the left-luggage places would be no good. She knows she's being watched.'

'Clever of you to find out so quickly, especially about her leaving some of the stuff in those envelopes.' Eddie looked up and something in Greg's expression told him that there was more in all this than he imagined. The bare bones of Grogan's story had been given – no details. 'It's awfully good of you to tell me, Greg. What can I say? But my God, supposing they raided the place before you found out.'

'Yes, and there might be a lot of publicity. She's planted

a few grains on other people too. They're all people who would not want that kind of publicity.' He paused and stared at his toes. 'Or any kind of publicity, Eddie.'

There was a long pause during which Eddie looked fixedly at the big man standing so awkwardly, his hands hanging by his side, one of them holding a glass, covering the top with his palm, the broad flat fingers gripping the sides. It was a picture Eddie was never to forget. Slowly Greg raised his head, and the two men looked at one another for a long moment.

'I see,' said Eddie quietly. 'I owe you more than I thought.'

'They're prepared to name names, drag a lot of things in, create a stink. Nobody wants that. But they're out to nail this gang, and they won't let anything stand in their way. It's bad enough as it is that she should be coming in and out of this house, but unless they grab her with the stuff on her, she could do a lot of damage. As it is, God knows what she's said.'

Eddie made one last effort. Understanding was one thing; words another.

'Well thanks to you she can't claim we've been buying the stuff from her. And if we can get into Paddy's room and clear that, if there's anything there ...'

'I'm not talking about that. But these things rub off. There could be talk, and if things really get dirty you might be called as witnesses. I don't think you will. But from what I hear this is a very clever gang operating from London. They know the set-up here. No scandals if we can help it. And that's just what they're playing on.'

Eddie knew now what was coming. This was the world breaking in, just as Maurice said it would.

'We'd better wait until Jim comes back,' he said playing for time. 'I certainly don't want him dragged into anything.'

'You may not be able to help it. Mud sometimes sticks.' He swallowed some whiskey a little too quickly, coughed and thumped his chest. 'Do you know a fellow called Gillespie, Eddie?' he said in a choked voice.

'Don't tell me he's in on the drugs racket too.'

Greg kept looking at the empty fireplace. Slowly, as if every word was being extracted like a tooth, he gave an account of what Grogan had told him.

Eddie listened, pale and tense, his body stunned by the shock. The police in Ireland are tolerant about most things – even drunken murderers were given surprisingly short sentences – but they are savage about the molestation of children. He was back in the jungle he had left so many years ago with Maurice. When Greg finished there was another silence. Neither men moved; and Eddie never knew how long it was until feeling came back in a hot rush of anger and shame.

'Well,' he said, unable to rise above a cliche, 'so now you know.'

'I've always known,' Greg said quietly.

'All those years,' Eddie thought of the welcoming little house in Dalkey, Dolly, with her startled and timid affection, and May, the strange gifted child whose attachment to him had become almost like a tie of blood since her mother's rescue. He felt a terrible wave of desolation. But the long years of polishing a social manner were good training: he managed to keep his voice fairly steady. 'I often wondered if you knew. I mean before ...' he could not bring himself to mention Maurice's name.

'That was different.'

A slow blush spread from the bottom of Greg's neck until his whole face was suffused. But instead of turning away he faced Eddie squarely, feeling his own particular anger. He had always been ashamed of his capacity for blushing, remembering how as a young rookie an unkind senior had christened him 'the gentle maiden'.

'Yes,' said Eddie softly, not without a touch of bitterness, 'and it was safe.'

'I didn't mean that,' said Greg roughly. 'It was none of my business, and I don't have to tell you what we owe to you, for Christ's sake. It was different because, because ...' he stopped and wiped his mouth with the back of his hand. 'You name it, you know what I mean. But this. Supposing

208

this fellow did the same again. Jesus. What would people say? What would they say about ...' he stopped and turned away, white-faced this time.

'Jim? Yes, I think I know what people would say, they're probably saying it already. Not that I care, not one single damn. But I don't want Jim dragged into it. He's not involved in any way whatever in this, I want you to know that. And if all these things broke over us, Jim would stand by us.' He took a step forward and stood near enough to Greg for the other to look at him defensively. 'This involves something else, something which all of us understand but don't want to – well – "name", as you said. It would have happened anyway, sometime. I've always known that. If this had been in Maurice's time, I'd have been grateful for what you've told me about the drugs, just as I'm grateful now. But in those days there wouldn't have been any other complications. No division. That's really what shocks you, isn't it?'

Greg furrowed his brows. He didn't quite follow. He had done his best, given his warning; but there was one thing he wanted, without quite knowing why, to be sure of. 'You mean Dillingham won't be involved?'

'I'll see that he isn't,' said Eddie gently. Then he turned away, and became suddenly brisk. 'Now I think I'd better ring Paddy up and get him to come back here at once.'

He went to the telephone and began to dial. Greg swallowed the rest of his drink in a gulp.

IX

Patrick Bellington was not one to prevaricate or ask unnecessary questions when his own interests were at stake. He drove straight back to Dublin after Eddie's telephone call and arrived at the square just before eleven. By this time Jim had come in and, accompanied by Greg, went up to his flat, took out *The Sacred Fount* and found another envelope between the pages of that ambiguous study of emotional cannibalism. Before he put it back he glanced at the last paragraph, and one sentence caught his eye. 'Such a last word – the word that put me altogether nowhere – was too unacceptable not to prescribe afresh that prompt test of escape to other air for which I had earlier in the evening seen so much reason.'

Jim tapped the book and looked at Eddie with a repressed smile. 'He gives no answers.'

'In a way he does. He leaves.' Eddie's voice was sad. So many clues, tangled threads, coincidences, vague hints of things imperfectly understood, positions taken up and the earth suddenly dissolving beneath them: life.

When Paddy arrived Eddie noticed that Jim seemed full of nervous energy, as if this brutal intrusion of the outside world had uncoiled something within him, forced a resolution, provided him with a ground for action to which he responded with a kind of oblique enthusiasm. The implications of the affair did not seem to trouble him in the least. After all, why should they? Eddie asked himself. The real problem lay much deeper than that.

Nothing was found in the top flat, although they searched it from end to end, even loosening floor boards, opening every one of the books, running their hands under the window-sills. At midnight they were all assembled in Jim's flat while Greg rang Grogan. He listened for quite a while before he put down the receiver.

"What did he say?" said Paddy anxiously. He was standing by the window, his hunched figure reflected in the glass. They had forgotten to draw the curtains.

'He thinks he may be on to something. There's someone at the party whose supply has been cut off for lack of cash. In the meantime he's glad you're all out of it.'

'But are we?' said Paddy, taking his hands out of his pockets and looking at them uselessly. 'I mean, am I?'

Greg gave him a look of faint dislike. The accent, the effeminate appearance, the obvious anxiety to have himself cleared at all costs were not calculated to soothe Greg's frayed nerves.

'That's your affair,' he said roughly. 'If you get yourself mixed up with a bitch like that you have to take the consequences.'

'But ...' Paddy began miserably and then turned away biting his lower lip. He looked like a small boy caught stealing the jam. This, thought Eddie unkindly, is where he longs for Nanny. Yet for the first time he felt himself regarding the man with sympathy. Perhaps his writing, meretricious though it was, meant more to him than just the money and publicity. And at the moment both of them were in very much the same boat. Eddie wondered idly if all sympathy was a transference of mutual difficulties.

'I think she's to be pitied,' put in Jim quietly, looking at Greg with a frown. He was sitting opposite Eddie holding the James novel on his lap like a breviary.

'Pitied!' Greg stared at him in surprise. 'And what about the people she's getting hooked on this poison?'

'They are to be pitied too. There are a great many factors the law cannot take into account. I think that's understood better here than in any other country, and the way you and Detective Grogan have acted tonight proves it. We're all right, Jack, yes. But how can anyone tell what goes on in the mind of that girl, or her victims? The most the law can do is preserve some sort of order, give some sort of protection. But it cannot really judge, any more than any of us can.'

Paddy turned around and was listening intently, Greg continued to stare silently, while Eddie, who was the first to look about the little circle, suddenly realized that Jim had taken over, was in command of the situation, and that

211

from now on whatever decisions were made would rest with him. He felt an immense sense of relief; a weight lifted from his own shoulders. He had thought that he himself would have to settle their accounts, a very one-sided affair brought to a head by a bizarre series of cloak and dagger events. Now they seemed to him almost irrelevant, a catalytic chain of events which had served their purpose. Maurice would have called it blind chance. Perhaps he was right.

Greg said nothing. He looked dead tired, the dark stubble of another day shading his chin and upper lip. Eddie felt his own unshaven cheeks, looked at the shadow on Jim's, the lighter growth on Paddy's. In a few hours the dawn would rise over the old sprawling, heedless city, stealing in across the bay like the viking founders, stirring the black pool with the pillage of light, flashing through the old streets, alleys and squares like an army of swords, as the beleaguered city rose to face another day. Or perhaps, so old, perverse and wileful was it, it would defeat the invading sun, summon up its mists and leave the pagan god with a tarnished blade, flourished ineffectually against a leaden sky.

'What am I going to do?' said Paddy pragmatically, looking at Jim before he turned to Greg.

'Say nothing, I suppose. If she finds out that we know about the plants, they may try something else. You'll just have to carry on as if nothing had happened, and search the flat every time she leaves. Don't ask her for the key, by the way. You'll know soon enough if she's nabbed.' He rubbed his forehead and sighed. 'I think I'd better be going home now. I told Dolly I'd be late, but she might wait up.'

'I'll ring for a taxi.' Eddie got up, his own reflection rising in the window pane in front of him: midnight and the doppelganger.

'I don't see why you should,' put in Jim quickly. 'The least we might do is take you home after what you've done for all of us. Eddie's got his car parked outside the door. I don't suppose any of us will sleep much tonight.'

Eddie looked at Jim gratefully. One of the things that occurred to him tonight was that Greg, now that he

212

had been forced out of his natural reticence into words which otherwise he would never have spoken, might not be able to get over his embarrassment, or ever be at ease with him again.

'No, no,' said Greg, reddening as Eddie looked at him, waiting for the verdict. 'That's too much trouble.' He was clearly confused by this turn of events.

'For an old friend?' Jim smiled. 'I don't think Eddie would agree. And if Dolly is sitting up she might make him a cup of tea.'

'We can do without the tea,' said Eddie briskly. 'Come on Greg. I'll go down and get the key.' He left the room before anything further could be said. Jim had brought off a fait accompli and Greg looked at him with a sort of baffled admiration. Then before he left to follow Eddie he said a curious thing.

'Good night, Father.'

'Good night, Greg, and thanks – for everything.'

Paddy, totally unaware of the treacherous currents beside which he had been standing, burst out petulantly when he found himself alone with Jim.

'What the hell am I going to do? This is awful. I'm quite sure that man thinks I'm in this up to my neck.'

'No, he doesn't. If I were you I'd go to bed, take a pill if you have one, and try to get some sleep. I'll wait until Eddie comes back.'

'So will I,' said Paddy pettishly.

'No, you won't.' Jim stood up and nodded towards the door. 'Go to bed, and ring up your wife first thing in the morning. Good night.'

213

X

It was nearly two o'clock when Eddie got back. As he locked his car he looked up and saw the lights still burning in Jim's flat, the curtains undrawn, and wondered at first if he had gone to sleep in his chair. Then he saw a tall figure standing at the window, waiting: a ghostly silhouette in the dark, silent facade of the square. He let himself in and went upstairs.

'How did things go?' Jim sat down and looked at the chair opposite. Before he accepted the implied invitation Eddie glanced at the bookcase. *The Sacred Fount* was back in its place. An episode closed, having served its purpose.

'Dolly was in bed, but she got up and made tea. We gave her an edited version of the story. So far as I'm concerned I suppose I always will.' Eddie sat down in the other arm chair and looked at Jim blankly.

'And Greg?'

'Careful, very careful. Very impressed by your attitude. That's what we spoke about going out. He'll always be grateful to me, of course, on account of Dolly. The very thing one doesn't want.' Eddie shook his head. In its own way and very differently from what he had intended, Maurice's warning was beginning to take shape.

'I don't blame him for being irritated by Bellington.' Jim looked up at the ceiling, and stroked the side of his nose. 'But why should he suddenly turn cop with you? His friend in the drugs squad must have made it quite clear to him that none of this is our fault.'

'I suppose he thinks we're a little bit too vulnerable. At least I am.' Eddie laid stress on the last words. They were intended to mean more than they said.

'We're all in this together.' Jim threw out a hand to include the whole house. 'Even the poor old La. If they don't succeed in pulling in this girl, and the gang who are behind her, Bellington is the only one who might

214

conceivably be implicated. She may give names, but she has no evidence now.'

'Greg is not interested in the others. Even if a scandal does break – and that's always possible even in Ireland – no one is going to take The La's part very seriously. The whole of Dublin knows she'd never have anything to do with a thing like that. And in the last resort Paddy would probably turn the whole affair to his own advantage. The publicity and so on. He's very clever at that.' Sitting very still, careful to make no movement Eddie approached the locked door: a thief in the night frozen into immobility by a faint warning sound, half-imagined, somewhere. In his case the remembered image in the upper room.

'I see.' Jim also remembered something: Greg's words as he went out.

'You might be tarred with my brush.' Eddie stroked the arm of his chair with his fingers, taking another step forward, determined on finishing the job in spite of creaking floor-boards. He noticed that his nails were dirty.

'He is very delicate.' Jim smiled with his eyes, and touched the back of the chair with his head: a sleeper awakening, listening for a moment, then relaxing. Nothing to worry about, just the familiar creaking of an old house he had grown to love, and would soon be leaving.

'Hardly that. He came out with some home truths. At least that's what a lot of people would call them.' Another step, and stillness. Or was there a faint sound of breathing?

'He will never understand you, for the simple reason that he doesn't really want to. Besides I suppose he thinks he has enough on his hands. But I think you can always rely on Dolly as a friend, if you want her. You have enough friends you can rely on. I'll stay until this drugs business is settled, no matter what happens.'

'You're leaving.' Eddie paused with his hand on the knob, with the sudden realization that he had been at this door before. It made the job a great deal easier. And there was no question in his voice: just a flat statement of fact. Farewells take place a long time before the trip to the station or the airport. A sudden death is the culmination of

215

a slow process through the veins, and the grand finale is always in the nature of an anti-climax: effective only in the theatre.

'I'm going to South America. It's the only thing left for me to do. Perhaps I can be of some use there. I'm not going as a priest, by the way, not in the beginning at any rate. I want to see how I'll fit in. There are social problems, lots of them, and I may be able to do something. But there's a hierarchy out there too. I may have to go underground. We'll see.' Jim's face was still and grave; the sleeper awakened, suspended between the dream, which had been interrupted and the prospect of rest.

'Underground? With a bishop?' Eddie smiled, opening the door noiselessly, pleased with his achievement. It had its element of farce, like all stealth.

'I think he'll stay overground.' Jim smiled, fully this time. The thief was in the room but the dreamer, half-awake, was remembering a joke. 'He proposed it, so he'll have to take the consequences. So I think I'll go with him, that is if this thing about the Vale girl is fixed up by then.'

Eddie paused, balancing himself, taking time to see with eyes accustomed to the dark, if there were any changes in the furniture of this familiar room.

'When does he intend to go?'

'August.' It was merely a creaking of springs.

'A month or more. Quite a lot can happen in that time.' Eddie rubbed both hands on the velvet of the armchair. His palms were damp. 'Greg had more news for me besides the drugs business.' This was the moment for fleeing, down the stairs and out into the night. He did not want this particular loot but it was his only way of living and besides, he had got into the habit of it. One ought to try and do a clean job, a vain hope, but even thieves have their pride which they flourish by throwing it away.

'What?' Jim sat up straight and looked at him. The light was suddenly switched on, and the sleeper, completely awake, confronted the intruder. 'I suspected there was something else. Greg would never have been that grim

216

about doing us a good turn. Are you in some kind of other trouble?'

There was a split second during which neither recognized the other. It was the same victim in the same room, and the last time he had got off relatively light.

'Not exactly what you think. I'm not being run in for indecent exposure, if that's what's on your mind. It's just that the company I keep is suspect.'

'I thought he might be.' The voice was slightly hard. One did not exactly welcome intruders in the night, even if the face was familiar and the person known to be non-violent. Nevertheless, now that the lights were on, and the unexpected visitor recognized as a person one had talked to all unwary in a dozen public places, there was a possibility that this could be worked out in a rational manner. 'What has he done?'

Eddie got up and moved behind the sofa. With his sweating hands clasped behind his back, staring at the clock on the mantelpiece, he told him. We have met before, mister, give me what you can afford and I won't trouble you again.

'What are you going to do?' said Jim. There was really no need for the questions, but it was reasonable to make sure that there were no hidden firearms.

'The right thing.' Eddie smiled cryptically, savouring the moment. Now that there was no further need for concealment, he was thrown back on his own resources; the outsider as a human being, engaged like most of the rest of the world in a thoroughly irrational argument which he himself invited. To rob the same room twice is tantamount to inviting sympathy for one's profession.

Jim raised his eyebrows. A moment of tension. The robbed have their secrets too, which they are only too glad to pay money to keep. A simple enough transaction, but essentially a collaboration.

'And Greg's definition of the right thing is predictable. He laid it on the line. Take my advice or keep away from my house. Not in so many words. But that's what it amounts to. And it makes you think twice about the

Hugheses.' Jim's voice was reasonable. There was nothing valuable in the room any more. The best pieces had been packed, stored, and were ready for shipment. He looked at the man behind the sofa with patient eyes.

'Not really.' Eddie looked at the lighted windows as if he were really a burglar, exposed to the view of any late passer-by. He saw his own reflection again; and was fully aware of his own nerve-ends. There wasn't much time but enough perhaps to justify himself. A pleasant job for an intruder who finds himself confronted with a sympathetic pigeon. 'Greg didn't express himself very well. I could do it better myself.'

'Perhaps it's just as well not to,' said Jim quietly. Was there any real need to explain to him that one could not have it both ways? Greg had known about Maurice and remained silent; accepting something which was deserving of respect. True and inexplicable, like all the worthwhile things in life. No doubt, given his limitations, he felt that his own devotion to Dolly was a finer thing; yet he accepted the other because of its simple reality. Then there had been no division and now there was. An arrangement which neatly divides the intellectual understanding of very close friends from a sensual entanglement based largely upon convenience, is somehow obscene. He could not explain to Jim that the absolute conviction of a total involvement was impossible between them, since Jim already knew it. In that respect Eddie realized better than anyone that he had been a thief. Better a frantic scandal with Abraham, giving everything, expecting little in return, than that.

'Yes,' said Eddie, prepared to accept whatever was offered. The loot was larger than he expected, but as he was to discover it contained one forged note.

'Listen, Eddie,' Jim's voice was urgent, a victim who realized that there was nothing between him and his despoiler except the force of circumstance. 'Do whatever you think right. I'm not worried about what people say, I've been through all that before. A lot of things can happen between now and August and I'm not tied to time. I can always put it off until later in the year.' This was generous. 'Have you anything in common with this fellow?'

Since Greg told him Eddie had had time to experience disgust, anger, even a touch of jealousy at what he now knew about Abraham. And indeed they had little enough in common. But at the moment he felt a twinge of defiance, a reaction, although he did not altogether realize it, against Jim's decision and evident ability to live alone.

'Yes,' he replied, 'I have.' Even with the friendliest of collaborators there was still honour among thieves.

Jim looked at him questioningly, doubt in his eyes. They asked a lot of things. What choice would be made, what would be the manner of it, above all could he too face the inevitable?

'In that case you'll have to ask him yourself. After all it's been a good many years. That doesn't make it any less horrible. But be careful, Eddie, please. Not because of me. But because ...'

'I know.' The message was clear. Take care of yourself. Don't be caught again. Next time there might not be such an easy getaway. In the meantime if you have to inhabit a half-world take my good wishes with you.

'Of course you may never want to see him again and it might be better not to. If you do, and find out that all this is old history, you may find that you can't throw him out just like that. And you may not want to. And anyway what's the use of asking questions. In the end it gets back to how we act.' Jim continued to look at him searchingly, and Eddie suddenly turned away and walked to the bookcase, looking blindly at the row of titles. He had just heard an echo of something he had recently said herself: I could analyze both of us out of existence and where would it get us? Back to where we are.

He did not know how long he stood there staring at the books, but when he turned back, quickly and without warning Jim was still looking at him, but the expression on his face had changed. It lasted hardly more than an instant; but it was enough to tell everything. The intruder had gone to the door, stopped to examine the loot and found the one forged note. What he saw mirrored in Jim's eyes, in the whole mould of his face with its sensitively controlled mouth, was something that he himself had been accused of only very recently. Pity.

That from the very beginning was what Jim had felt for him; and that was why he had always held back from this man who bore such a troubling resemblance to Maurice. But Maurice had no pity. Only love, and where there is that, there is no room for the minor emotions, above all for this awful shadow of something hard, uncompromising and inexplicable.

But he made one last effort. After all the note had been planted on the victim too. Somewhere along the line he too had been cheated.

As if he realized that something had happened and that he might be called upon to make restitution, Jim stood up and made a slight vague gesture with his hands. Perhaps he felt that he had been discovered in a weakness at a time when he could afford to show none.

'Stay here tonight,' he said quietly. 'I don't think either of us feel like going to bed. We'll sit and drink.'

'I could do with one.' Eddie came back from the bookcase and sat down on the sofa. Another echo, almost too painful to remember. 'Stay with me tonight. Please.' Then there had been justice. This was justice of another kind. The intruder was invited to stay, his little theft tacitly forgiven and the understanding offered that no questions would be asked. And when the morning came he would slip away, grateful after his own fashion that farewell was implicit in the offer and the acceptance. When the time for parting came there would be no need for words. An unusual encounter between different worlds which neither would forget.

They settled down with two large glasses of brandy and talked: of Jim's still unsettled plans, of The La, Grace and Desmond, Paddy and Kate Vale: the sort of easy, unaffected exchange that might have prevailed if they had been two different people, and which was possible now only at the moment of parting, when both of them accepted each other for what they were instead of what they might have been.

Dawn came with a dry little chuckle, and a curious muffled flutter of wings as the sparrows under the eaves ruffled their nests. Light came slow, for during the night clouds had moved in from the west and the city resisted the disturber of its dreams. It came, the invader from the east, like a sapper in a camouflage suit, creeping on his belly over enemy territory cutting barbed wire, then melting into the landscape as the battalion moved up behind him. Only some of them got through. There was no slow pink invasion of streets, alleys and parks, only a dull easing of the dark sky into a sort of flannel grey. Another stalemate in which the sun was afforded no triumphal march in that devious place.

As Eddie stood by the window looking out across the square he thought of Dublin, his second home, which he loved a little and did not particularly hate. It was like a very old lady, once beautiful and still handsome, who was now suffering from a malignant tumour which disfigured one side of her face. Sometimes she covered it up and displayed her still unblemished profile in a soft becoming light. He thought of certain haunted streets, doorways, corners of squares, a sudden vista of pale houses, the colour of fine old skin mantled with pink. At other times the old crone would turn and reveal her awful swelling with a malicious cackle of defiance at the transitory fumblings of all human effort. At this time of the morning the towers of Ballymun must look like an ancient, ill-fated settlement built and abandoned by some barbaric tribe, a sight of sinister glory, while the other and more pretentious concrete developments of the centre and suburbs were swollen with an ambiguous light.

But Eddie, as he turned away and looked at Jim standing beside him, remembered other dawns in other cities when he had identified his emotion, sad or joyful, with bricks, stones and a hopeful glimmer of sun. He knew better now.

'Another day,' said Jim, rubbing his blue beard.

'Yes,' said Eddie, accepting it.

221